THE BLUE GONFALON

The Blue Gonfalon

MARGARET ANN HUBBARD

ILLUSTRATED BY SHANE MILLER

1960

DOUBLEDAY & COMPANY, INC.

GARDEN CITY, NEW YORK

Library of Congress Catalog Card Number 60–8873

To Godfrey's dear friend and mine,
Florence Melander

CONTENTS

THE BLUE GONFALON

CHAPTER ONE
THE POACHER

The rain itself made more noise than Bennet. High up in the lofty awnings formed by the pines the dripping began, coming down branch by branch until it fell finally in leathery plops all over the forest floor. Bennet was barefooted and his doublet was as soaked as the cedars, so he made no sound whatever as he slipped through the underbrush. The worst trouble he had was to keep from laughing because Old Barb looked so funny up ahead, hopping along lopsided as if he were constantly jumping over puddles. He had walked that way ever since he had come back from Rome with the lance wound in his thigh. The wound had healed badly—Lord Godfrey had said it was a miracle it had healed at all, the way Old Barb lived—but it hadn't slowed him down. He was still the craftiest poacher in the whole Ardennes Forest.

That was why Bennet was so jubilant over catching him red-handed. With four rabbits slung on his back, his stout slingshot looped over his shoulder and a couple of snares in his hand, Barb would have quite a chore convincing the sheriff that he was merely out for a stroll. Not that Bennet had any intention of getting the sheriff. By the time he'd run clear back to the castle, hunt up a marshal or a bailiff and be back here, Old Barb would have disappeared like a magician's trick. He could smell danger, he had often told Bennet, better than a fawn sniffing the wind for its mother.

Only not right now. He was a little too confident of being alone. Although the woods had opened out into a fairy-sized meadow, the old fellow never stopped to glance around, a mistake Bennet would be happy to point out to him later. The enormous cap he wore looked like a complete animal, bobbing along. He had made it out of the whole skin of a kid with the little hoofs dangling at the back and the weather-beaten tail sticking up on top. His own shaggy white hair straggled out like part of the matted fur. His breeches and short tunic were of leather, either tanned by himself or stolen from the tannery, dark now from the wet. Even with the woods still in the bareness of early spring, Old Barb was so forest-colored he'd be invisible in the thicket. Catch him now, Bennet decided, don't take a chance.

Holding back his laughter, rolling soundlessly heel to toe as Old Barb had taught him, the boy loped through the soggy grass. Only a few yards away from the hurrying old gnome, he stopped.

"Your rabbits or your life!" he shouted.

Old Barb spun around so swiftly that the little hoofs made a clatter, his toothless mouth dropped open and the bushy eyebrows flew almost up under the cap. The rabbits slid to the ground. Bennet let out a roar of laughter.

"Now who's the smartest tracker, you or me?" Bennet demanded in small coughs because he couldn't stop laughing. "You didn't hear me, Barb! You didn't even know I was behind you!"

"Of course I didn't!" the old fellow snapped. "Who taught you, anyway?"

"I caught you fair and square so I deserve the credit!"

"Credit nothing!" Barb's thin jaw chopped as if he were chewing something very fast. He always did that when he was angry. "And don't yell. You want to bring every marshal in Bouillon on the run?"

"I don't care who comes! I haven't done anything wrong!" And in his hilarity Bennet fell to his knees, doubled over in the wet grass.

He knew afterward that he couldn't have been hunched down that way very long before he heard the thump of feet —the space of several breaths, possibly. The sound was alarming because only robbers and poachers came this deep into the forest. And a marshal, Edmond. He came sprinting out through the skimpy foliage, a stocky man in the blue livery of Bouillon, his face swollen red. Bennet was a little sorry. It was one thing to make a game of catching Old Barb but something very different to have Edmond come along. Poaching could be punishable by death if the lord of the manor decided so. Lord Godfrey never meted out such a sentence except for murder or highway robbery. But Barb, an old offender in the forest, could well be thrown into the dungeon and forgotten.

Bennet came slowly to his feet. Edmond, puffing, pointed at a spot beyond.

"What's that? Rabbits, are they? So you've been poaching!"

"*Me?*" Bennet squeaked. His voice was changing and he never knew how it was going to come out. Slowly he turned, feeling prickles run up under his curly mop and right down his snub nose as if the freckles were dancing. The place where Old Barb had stood was empty. Empty, except for a limp heap of rabbits.

"The old barbarian, I suppose he caught them?" the marshal scoffed. "He gets blamed for everything. Where are your snares?"

"I haven't got any snares!"

Edmond pushed Bennet aside. Scuffling his foot through the wet grass, his foot came hard against a hidden rock and he howled at the sharp pain. Balancing on one leg, he pressed the hurt toe in his hand.

"You're the armorer's boy, aren't you? Josef's son?"

"Yes, sir. I'm Bennet."

"Josef's an honest man. Hasn't he taught you to tell the truth?"

"Yes, sir."

"Then let's have it! Where are the snares?"

In the pouch fastened to Old Barb's belt—how could Bennet say that?

"If the old man caught the rabbits, he wanted them to eat," Edmond sputtered on. "Well, then, why did he dump them here?"

Because he heard you coming, and I didn't. Bennet couldn't say that either. He stared at Edmond's good foot in the soaked shoe. What wouldn't he give to tramp on it hard so it would hurt like the other one, then race off through the woods so fast that no fat marshal ever would catch him!

"Pick up the rabbits and let's be on our way," Edmond ordered, trying his foot gingerly on the ground. "Walk ahead of me. And no tricks! If you escape I'll summon the archers to hunt you. Straight, now!"

Bennet took hold of the leather thong—no doubt stolen from the tanner—and swung the rabbits to his back. He hated the feel of the soft, dead things. He never had the heart to kill. Watch the animals in the woods, follow them to their dens, lie so still against a log that a little striped skunk would sidle over to him, that was what he loved doing. But not killing.

The marshal had difficulty in keeping up the pace, but Bennet was not concerned for him. He was sick over the thought of having Lord Godfrey know that the son of a member of his household had fallen so low. The Duke of Lorraine was the perfect knight, all of France knew that. Although it had happened when the knight was very young, the story was still told in the armory of how he had been chosen by every tongue to bear the standard of the emperor Henry IV in the decisive battle on the Elster, and he had struck the rival emperor, Rodolf, so furiously with the staff of the banner that Rodolf died a few days later. When Henry needed an army again to march against Pope Gregory VII, Godfrey gathered his forces and was the first to scale the walls of Rome. He had regretted this feat, however, for he was often heard to say that no man should take up arms against the Holy Father. The emperor had given him as reward the territory of Antwerp and the Duchy of Lorraine, making him as powerful as the king of France, but Godfrey took no pleasure in his possessions. He was still worried about the sacrilege of storming Rome. Wrongdoing in any degree had become repellent to him. And poaching, Bennet thought sadly, was not a small misdemeanor. The master would be sorely disappointed in this son of his faithful armorer. Bennet had no defense. What would his word be worth against Edmond's?

The sun came out and the woods began to steam with an earthy freshness. The long grassy slope crowned by the castle would have been delightful to climb in happier circumstances, for all across it birds were flying up, singing, and grasshoppers were shuttling back and forth. Through the past century, ever since the great stone stronghold had been heaped on the bluff by Godfrey's forefathers, armies of warring barons had stormed up the slope from time to time, shot their stones and arrows against the walls and found them impregnable. Bennet had always seen the castle in the proud light of a possession because in his heart he had sworn fealty to Master Godfrey as his liege lord. Now, with the illegal rabbits on his back, weighed down by the anger of injustice, he saw the mighty battlements as the defeated armies had seen them, impregnable, dark as a prison keep. Even the blue banners flipping themselves dry atop the towers were like tongues stuck out in ridicule.

The sunshine had wakened more than the birds and the grasshoppers. As Bennet approached the gate a half dozen of the younger pages rode out on their small gentle palfreys, took one look at the rabbits and the marshal and swung the horses into a tangled pack in their panic to be first inside with the news. A few ducks in a puddle cocked their heads, quacking. In the courtyard another quacking started, the pages' high-pitched shouts. Deeper voices answered, a few laughs, questions. Poaching? *Josef's* son?

With head hanging, Bennet trudged into the sunshine of the bailey. Not only had a good number of knights assembled

with more joining them, but the tall figure of Lord Godfrey
himself was just emerging from the armory with Josef following behind. Godfrey stopped short, a frown on his handsome
face, his arms folded, his feet apart as he might have stood
on the wall of Rome. The wind lifted his light brown hair
from his shoulders, the sun deepened the blue of his tunic
and shot bars of light from the silver belt hung with medallions. Bennet came to a stop a few paces off and the rabbits
fell with a limp plop against his ankles.

"What's this, Bennet?" Godfrey asked incredulously.

"Poaching, my lord!" Edmond declared. His chest was
high and his ruddy face glowing with importance. "I caught
him fairly!"

"What was he doing? Why, he was running with the
rabbits on his back!"

Bennet's head snapped up. Before he could protest, Godfrey asked in the same quiet tone, "Was he?"

"Well—he was standing there on the path, but he'd been
running!"

"Where were the rabbits?"

"On the ground beside him."

"How far away?"

"A foot or two, Sire."

"How far?"

"I don't see what difference it makes, my lord! They were
there and he was there!"

"Is that the truth, Bennet?"

Bennet was too near to unmanly tears of anger to do more
than nod.

"Did you catch the rabbits?"

"No, Sire, I did not!"

"Very well. André! Take these things to the kitchen. We
don't have to waste the fresh meat. Now, Josef, I'll show you

where I was thinking of setting up a new quintaine for the pages——"

"But—but, my lord——" Edmond sputtered.

"Yes?" The look Lord Godfrey fastened on Edmond was cold and still.

"My lord, *somebody* caught the rabbits!"

"Undoubtedly. But that isn't Bennet's concern."

"Well—no! But it's mine!"

"Then find out who did it," Godfrey said, and turned away as if the matter were ended.

A ripple of amusement breezed through the crowd, which was a sizable gathering since by now everyone within running distance had arrived. Edmond, very red in the face, blustered off. Little André, shouting to the other pages to wait for him, dragged the rabbits toward the kitchen. Josef gave his son a long regard before he limped after Lord Godfrey. He was a small man, bowed even shorter by the years he had spent bending over a forge in the blacksmith shop, lame from sitting with one leg curled under him while he oiled mail in the armory. The look promised he would get the truth out of his son about the poaching incident, and then there would be another long lecture about the dangers of running with Old Barb.

"I don't care," Bennet muttered. "I don't care about anything as long as Lord Godfrey believed me!"

"It doesn't make much difference," a clear voice said close beside him. "You're not a page anyway."

Bennet whirled, his fists hard. Leroy, tall and lithe, stood with arms folded in good imitation of Lord Godfrey, his curly black head well up, smiling with his superior air. Leroy never let anyone forget that he was the nephew of the Duke of Normandy. He had eyes as blue as the livery he kept so clean, and he had a voice which with its sweetness could draw exclamations of delight from the ladies or goad his fellow pages into fist fights for which he never was blamed.

"You'll never be a page, or a squire or a knight," Leroy went on, his soft leather shoe stroking a cobblestone. "Too bad you were born the son of a peasant, but there's nothing you can do about it, is there?"

A couple of knights had turned, listening in astonishment. Leroy was usually very certain that his baiting would not be overheard, but he hadn't been able to pass up so perfect a chance to aim a dart at his favorite target. Bennet knew why this young nobleman enjoyed cuffing him down. It was because he could leap to the back of a horse faster than Leroy, he could run longer distances without getting winded, he could turn more somersaults down the long slope behind the castle. Only a few days ago, when the pages had gathered noisily in the armory and were challenging one another to feats of skill, Bennet had darned a heavy shirt of chain armor and danced in it until Leroy reminded them all that the peasant had no business sharing the sports of the nobility, and they had been forced to run him out. Leroy had been more overbearing than ever since then.

Bennet glanced at the knights who stood watching. They knew what Leroy had said. But Bennet would have to be the one to start the fight and he was already in enough trouble. Wheeling, he ran across the bailey and out through the Great Gate, to plunge into the brambles surrounding the castle wall. It felt good to fight something. Scraped and scratched, he came out finally on the precipice above the river.

The Semois was always quiet as it flowed past the village of Bouillon. After the rain it was a clay-colored road. Down by the water the huts stood thickly together, scattering up the lower slope as high as they could cling, a motley gathering of homes and the shops of the silversmiths, tanners, wheelwrights, and other tradesmen who served the castle. In the willows by the water children shouted and dogs barked. Bennet stared glumly down at his own home, a log house propped against the cliff by means of stout pilings. On its thatched roof a cat sat eating something, probably a mouse she had caught in the straw.

Bennet knew he should get home before the news of his escapade could reach Mama. But he plunked himself down on a rock and scooped up a handful of wet clay. He worked hard at it for a while, forming a head that to him looked exactly like Leroy. Then he stood up and took a great deal of pleasure out of smashing it flat with his heel. After that he scowled down again at the cat who was now washing her face. Then in long leaps he plunged down the path.

Mama was kneading bread in the flour trough when Bennet, having scattered the chickens in the dooryard, rushed into the house. She turned and brushed back her hair with her elbow, and her mouth was tight. Antoine, who was six, had evidently been telling her something, for he hung his head and sidled around Bennet toward the door. All Bennet could do at the moment was to make a threatening face at him.

"I needed flour from the mill, but you weren't to be found, no," Mama said. "I had to send Antoine and Arabelle for enough to make the loaves."

"I'll get you some more, Mama. Right away." And Bennet made a lunge for the doorway.

But Violette was not the one to let her children off easily.

"Bennet! What is this Antoine tells me about you getting caught by the marshal?"

Bennet let out a long breath as he turned to his mother. She wore a rough wool sack for a dress and she stood barefooted on a dirt floor, but from her sons and daughters she commanded respect.

"Answer me, Bennet!"

"It was nothing, Mama. I was tracking Old Barb and he had a catch of rabbits, and when Edmond came along he dropped them and—well, Edmond thought I was the poacher. That's all."

"That's all! This is nothing that you are a poacher!"

"But I'm not, Mama, I hadn't——"

Violette caught her son by the ear and sat him down hard on the bench by the table. The younger children who had been peeking around the door suddenly disappeared.

"So you have been running wild in the woods again with that old barbarian!"

"But Mama, I——"

"Would you have been caught if you weren't there?"

Bennet shook his head carefully. He would have liked to lay his hand over his smarting ear, but that might remind Mama that she had not boxed the other one.

"I didn't do anything bad, Mama. I don't copy Old Barb. I just like to learn about the woods from him, about how to track and where the animals drink and how you can catch fish by dropping a certain bark on the water, things like that."

"You need to know how to catch the fish for you to be a priest?"

This was old ground and Bennet had to make an effort to be patiently respectful.

"I am not going to be a priest, Mama."

"No? Then you will be an armorer, like your father?"

"No, Mama."

"No, no, no! Always it is no, Mama! Then what will you be?" But before he could answer, she held up her floury hand. "I know, a knight! It makes no difference that you must be nobly born to be a knight, that you must be taken into a nobleman's household at the age of seven to become a page——" Violette narrowed her eyes at her son. "Do you realize you're fourteen now, the age to be made a squire if you were going to be a knight? And what are you? Nothing!"

Bennet watched his mother reach for the gourd of grease and begin clapping a coating on the coarse, dark mound of dough.

"For the son of a peasant there are but two things to be, a priest or a tradesman, unless he wants to till the soil," Violette went on. "In the priesthood a man can better himself; he can help his brothers to better things, find good husbands for his sisters, support his parents in their old age. He can go from the monastery to the chair of the Pope like our great Urban! But for you, no! Because you cannot be a knight you will be nothing!"

Bennet knew his mother spoke wisely. Once in a while a peasant's son was knighted because of his own deeds of courage or because a nobleman owed a debt of gratitude to the father. But Lord Godfrey owed Papa no debt of gratitude, and a deed of courage could not be performed unless the opportunity presented itself.

"Mama," Bennet said slowly, and he got up and went over to lean on the bread trough beside Violette. "Mama, one reason why I want to be a knight——"

"Is what, yes?"

"Is I want to buy you some silk for a dress."

"Fine! A silk dress is what I need, like Godfrey's lady!"

But Mama's hard countenance relaxed and she looked at Bennet as if she saw something new in him. She would never show affection toward her children. Gentleness was a thing she knew little about.

"A silk dress," she said. "It would be nice."

Her touch was light as she tucked the linen towel over the bread to keep it warm for rising.

Bennet poked a finger into the flour, withdrew it and watched the hole close up. He wanted Mama to be satisfied with him, even proud. But he was not going to be either a priest or a tradesman even to please her.

CHAPTER TWO
KU-KU PETER

Young Tancred, nephew of the Prince of Tarentum, did not know he was doing a favor for the son of a peasant when he led his knights breakneck up the long slope to Bouillon Castle, thundered over the bridge, and drew his mount to a rearing halt in the bailey. All of his company were as young as he, a noisy, laughing crowd met by Duke Godfrey and his knights with a boisterous welcome. Tancred and his youthful followers, proving their mettle as bearers of the

sword, had ridden up far into Normandy and now over into
the Ardennes Forest, and all their chain mail needed oiling
and the spurs sharpening and the silver medallions a good
polishing. And that was where the favor to Bennet came in:
Josef, in charge of the armory, worked early and late to accommodate the demands of the guests. He had no time even
to remember that his son not only had been caught running
around with Old Barb but had been practically taken in the
act of poaching.

Bennet, keeping in the background, mingled with the
crowd which always surrounded the newcomers. The tales
of their travels were fascinating, the songs they sang so new
that no one could even hum along with them. Tancred, only
seventeen, with the beard on his cheeks still pale thistle-
down, was broad of shoulder and tall. His blond hair, cut
short in the new fashion, gleamed around his head in a curling crown. In the impromptu tournaments staged by the
knights out on the jousting field, Tancred unhorsed every
opponent. He had wanted to be a monk, the squires reported, but his swashbuckling uncle, Bohemund who was
Prince of Tarentum, had convinced him that a knight could
do as much for God as a priest. The calmness of spirit that
would have been so fitting in a monastery gave him a charm
that Bennet loved. The tow-headed, barefoot boy in the
leather jerkin was never far away from the young knight,
and no one ever told him to be off.

Early in the afternoon of the third day, however, Bennet's
good luck ended. Hidden behind a great oil cask in the
armory, he was watching Tancred and his knights testing
a new array of javelins when his father caught sight of him.

"Bennet? Come here! Take these spurs down to the silversmith. Tell him to repair them and have them back by morning, ready for my lord Tancred."

Bennet caught up the spurs and ran. Delightful as it was to be entrusted with the beautiful golden spurs Tancred had received when he was knighted, the boy didn't want to miss the javelin throwing that would soon be taking place out on the jousting field. He raced across the bailey and out of the Great Gate, around the wall, and went sliding and jumping down the steep path.

Something unusual was taking place down on the river-bank. Every man, woman, child, and dog in the village appeared to be assembled on the water's edge. A wandering minstrel must have stopped by, or a magician with a dancing bear. But there was no sound of music. As he drew nearer Bennet could see that the people were intently listen-ing to a small man who was speaking to them from a rather risky perch atop a stump. Such incidents were so rare in the village that nobody could be censured for stopping a minute. And perhaps the silversmith himself was somewhere under the willows. With the gold spurs tight in his hand, Bennet joined the crowd.

The speaker was the thinnest man Bennet ever had seen. He wore a woolen robe tied around the waist with a rope, and he had a sort of monk's hood falling loose over his shoulders. Even his hair was sparse and of no color at all until it tangled with the dull red beard. His face and arms, his thin shanks and bare feet were browned to the hue of old wood. Propped in his hand was a large cross crudely fashioned from the un-peeled limbs of a tree. At the edge of the crowd dozed a mule idly switching his half-bare tail at the flies.

"I've seen it!" the little man cried in a high voice which broke with passion, and his fiery black eyes raked the crowd and his fist shook until you could almost hear the bones rattle. "I was there when the infidels jumped on the altar to distract the faithful from prayer! I saw them spill the holy water and splinter the candles burning at the sepulchre of Our Lord! And I tell you, God will grant no favors to the Christian world so long as such sins are permitted!"

He paused to wipe a riffle of foam from his lips.

"Who is he?" Bennet asked Victor, the tanner, beside him.

"Ku-ku Peter."

"Who?"

"He's a hermit."

"What's he talking about?"

"The Holy Land."

"Why?"

"Listen!"

"What does Ku-ku mean?"

"It's a Picard word. Little. Now be quiet!"

Other people were turning their heads in annoyance, but Bennet had to know one more thing.

"Where did he come from?"

"I don't know. Jerusalem."

"What was he doing there?"

The tanner fingered the stick with which he had been stirring dye, and Bennet subsided. Ku-ku Peter was going on a little more calmly.

"It was different in olden times. Jerusalem was sacred to the Moslems as well as to the Christians because it is the site of their Mosque of Omar, and they came side by side with the pilgrims from the West to visit their own holy places. When the great numbers of Christians flocked to Jerusalem to see the end of the world in the year one thousand, and the Moslems decided to make some money by charging a byzant to enter the city gates, that was all right. No one minded the small sum. But now the Turks have taken the Holy Land from the Moslems! They have overrun Palestine clear to the borders of Egypt and they heap insults and injuries on the pilgrims! Priests are beaten, women and children are stolen and sold into slavery, men are tortured and imprisoned. But worse than this——" He paused, gathering breath, and his thin voice rang out. "Worse far than this are the sacrileges they commit! We cannot leave the Holy Places in the hands of the Turks! We must avenge the Lord!"

"Yea!" The long shout was like a sigh, answering Peter. Before it could die, the little man stooped forward confidentially.

"I'll tell you what happened to me. In the year 1093, only two short years ago, I made a pilgrimage to Jerusalem. There I was sickened by the things I saw. So I went to the patriarch of Jerusalem, Simeon, and we wept together even as Christ wept over the fate of the city! Who can save it from the infidel, we asked each other. Not the Christians of the Orient, for their sins are too heavy. Not the Greeks, for they are occupied in trying to keep together their empire. So who must make up the armies of the Lord? You—and me! The Christians of the West! You, men! You, women and children! No one is exempt! We'll march to save Jerusalem! All of us together, for God!"

Many of the women were crying now, not knowing they did so. Bennet hugged the spurs in both arms until the rowels pricked his chest.

"God spoke to me," Peter continued. "Right out of His own sepulchre He spoke to me! My last night in Jerusalem I was kneeling in prayer in the Church of the Resurrection, begging God to show me how this great crusade could be accomplished. And I fell asleep, and in my dream Christ appeared in shining garments, and He said to me, 'Arise, Peter, arise! Be not afraid! I will be with thee in whatever thou shalt undertake, for the time has come that My sanctuary shall be cleansed and the clean fire lighted for

all the world to see! Through you I will have mercy on My
city and deliver it back to My own people!'" Slowly Peter's
arms fell to his sides and his gaze burned over the crowd.
"That was His promise to me—and to *you!* Are you with
me?"

"Amen!" an old man shouted. Others took up the shout
until the amens rang through the willows.

"When do we go?" a young voice cried.

"When all of France is awakened! France is the hope
of the Holy Land!"

A grumbling began, and Peter spread his hands for
silence.

"I know, my friends, I know how you long to pick up
a lance and charge away tomorrow. But listen. When I
left Jerusalem I went straight to Rome, where I was received
by our beloved Pope. And that in itself was a mark of God's
favor, for why else should the great Urban II listen for a
whole morning to a humble monk? And he not only listened,
but he commanded me to travel all through France, for
there live the people who would hear me, he said. And
when there are great enough numbers for a mighty army,
then together we will march to Jerusalem!"

The shouts and acclaim were deafening, people sobbed
with emotion, and there were cries of "He is a saint!" Using
the rude crucifix as a crutch, the little man leaped off the
stump. Immediately he was caught up and lifted shoulder
high, and so he appeared to be floating on top of the crowd.
Bennet felt as if he floated with Peter, furious, vengeful,
brave, ready to accomplish anything. If only Lord Godfrey
were to hear Peter's message! Why, he would lead the whole
crusade!

Bennet tried to nudge into the crowd.

"Ahoy, now, we're not a bunch of Turks!" an old fellow complained. "Don't claw us, boy!"

"Then let me through! I've got to get through!"

All the arms were upraised, reaching for Peter, and Bennet put his head down and squirmed along. When finally he raised up to see where he was, one of the monk's bare feet met him in the face. He grabbed the foot, pulling.

"Easy, easy, son!" Peter cried. "Don't pull me apart!"

"Then listen to me! You've got to listen!"

"Halt, everyone! Let me hear the boy."

The crowd quieted. Bennet still clung to the foot.

"Come up to the castle, sir—please! Lord Godfrey will go with you to the Holy Land!"

"I don't visit castles, son."

"But how can Lord Godfrey help if he doesn't know about the crusade?"

The old man shook his grizzled head. "My message will find its way into the halls of the nobles without me."

"The boy is right, somebody has to lead us!" the tanner cried.

"Then hush and I will tell you who our leader will be." When the quiet was broken only by the quacking of a few ducks, Peter raised the cross high. "He will be none other than the Holy Father himself!"

A gasp ran over the crowd. "Urban? The Pope?"

"Urban is a Frenchman, he went to Rome from our own monastery of Cluny. He knows the heart of France. Not many months will pass before he returns to preach the crusade! Urban himself will lead the army!"

The shouting broke into an ovation. Once more the eager arms reached for Peter and he was tossed away across the crowd to be set down finally beside his mule. The animal woke up and began to back nervously, for all over France people had been pulling hairs from his tail as souvenirs and it was sore and plucked nearly bare.

Bennet tried to fight his way after Peter but everyone else had the same intention. Circling out around the ducks which had somehow been caught up in the general movement, he raced on to the point where the road twisted up the steep riverbank. Planting himself firmly, he waited for the scrambling mass to meet him.

"Out of the way, boy!" the tanner shouted.

But Bennet only dug his toes into the clay. Jostled and shoved, he stood his ground. The trick worked. The ranks had to part to go around him and he met Peter and the mule head on. Then, clinging to the mule's neck, happily shouting with the rest, he tramped on deep into the forest.

The late sunlight was filtering through the beeches before Bennet realized where he was. The gold spurs were still clutched in his hand! What would Papa say now? Although the boy ran all the way back to the village, it was sunset before he went jumping and sliding again down the path to the river. In the twilight he found the silversmith and delivered the spurs. Then, disregarding the thought of Mama watching the path and wondering what could be keeping him this time, he climbed the bluff to the castle.

"My message will find its way into the halls of the nobles without me," Peter had said. Bennet was not exactly carrying the message. News of so great and holy a purpose would not be entrusted to a boy. But he was going to listen to the conversation in the Great Hall tonight when all the guests and the household gathered for supper, and he would know if anyone at all had heard Ku-ku Peter. And he knew exactly where he could hide for the best listening.

As Bennet had hoped, nobody noticed him hidden in the

drapery of the wide doorway. The velvet curtain had been
looped back for the convenience of the servants, and from
its folds he could see easily into the Great Hall. Supper at
Bouillon Castle was equal to a banquet anywhere else. At
the longest table Lord Godfrey sat in his enormous chair
with his squire behind him to see that he was well served
and Leroy, of course, to attend the squire. That was the
only bad feature of the hidingplace. The master's table, and
therefore Leroy, was only a few feet away. There were
guests tonight at Godfrey's board, handsome noblemen in
rich attire, each served by a squire and pages. Madame
presided at the other long table, entertaining the wives and
daughters of the visitors. There were several shorter tables,
but even the smallest seated a dozen men. Candles were
aflame in the sconces around the walls, and between them
hung the armor of departed warriors like shells of the dead
men, complete even to the helmets. Crossed lances and
banners, old Roman battle-axes and new Norman swords
all decorated the walls. In the soft light the women's jewels
sparkled, silk shone richly, silver bracelets gleamed as a
knight reached for his goblet. Behind the chairs the squires
in their bright-colored livery and the pages in their masters'
colors were like brilliant birds hovering.

Bennet's eyes rested longest, as always, on Lord Godfrey.
His smooth light brown hair was made gold by the candles
behind him. Other knights ate with a bone in both hands,
gnawing away with no better manners than the dogs slink-
ing under the tables. But Master Godfrey ate delicately,
dipping his fingers often in the bowl of warm water beside
his trencher. And still he was not a womanish knight. In
courage and resourcefulness he was never equaled in battle.
What a leader for the crusade!

"What's this?" the master of the pantry suddenly cried,

and Bennet ducked out of sight. But the pantryman was not
remarking the unusual bulkiness of the drapery. He had
caught a kitchen boy sneaking around for a glimpse of the
guests, and it was several minutes before Bennet dared
move again. The rich smell of the roasted meat was driving
him frantic with hunger. If nobody mentioned Ku-ku Peter
soon, he'd watch his chance and sprint to the scullery where
Hughette could be depended upon to slip him something to
eat.

The diners had now reached the stage of nibbling the nut
cakes, and conversation was lively.

"He's a hermit of some kind, a monk," Tancred was saying. "I've heard he has a wife but he left her years ago.
He's just back from the Holy Land."

"What's his name, Tancred?"

"Ku-ku Peter is what they call him."

"Coo coo, like the doves?"

Laughter ran through the hall. Tancred leaped to his feet.
Bennet could see him past the corner of Lord Godfrey's
chair, splendid in green with a great deal of gold embroidery,
his curly crown shining in the candlelight.

"All right, laugh if you will! The hermit is not a voice crying in the wilderness! He went to Jerusalem and returned
safely! And others have done it, too! Look!"

He swung his arm dramatically toward the wall beside
Bennet, and the lining of his cape shone red. The boy
hastily swung the curtain around himself. He knew what
Tancred meant. The dried and curled palm leaves on the
wall had been brought back from the Holy Land by someone who ever afterward received the name of palmer.

"Remember, Tancred," Lord Godfrey said quietly, "remember there is a great difference between the passage of
a few thousand pilgrims and the movement of armed men.

The very sight of armored knights would provoke assault. Why shed the blood of innocent people?"

"Christ Himself was innocent of sin; yet He shed His blood for us, who are unworthy. Why should we hold our lives more precious than His?"

The laughter died. Tancred's handsome face glowed as he turned to his audience again. Quietly Bennet turned until once again he could see the assemblage.

"If you could hear the hermit tell it, how the infidels spit and stamp on the altars, defile the very place where Our Lord's body lay in the sepulchre, tramp along the Way of the Cross—but who among you heard Peter today?"

"I did!"

Bennet's answer rang out on the heels of Tancred's question. He hadn't known he was going to speak. But suddenly there it was, a shrill cry hanging in the sudden silence. People looked around in bewilderment, wondering who had spoken. Lord Godfrey had turned in his great chair and his gray eyes had gone straight to the culprit, the uncombed, freckle-faced, bodiless head protruding from the folds of the curtain.

Bennet knew his face flushed as red as the curtain, for he could feel the heat. To add to his embarrassment, everyone saw him now; and Lord Godfrey was biting the inside of his cheeks to keep from laughing. The master of the pantry, who fancied himself to be the overlord of the Great Hall, bustled forward sputtering, but Lord Godfrey held up his hand.

"Let him come out, Louis."

The master stopped. Bennet stood like a statue inside the curtain. Everyone waited. Laurent spoke to Leroy, and the young nobleman drew away the curtain as if he were touching something not very nice.

Godfrey permitted himself to smile now. "That's better—why, it's Josef's son! What do you know about Ku-ku Peter?"

"I heard him, Sire, in the village. Today."

"And what did he say?"

"Just what Monsieur Tancred has told you, sir, all about the infidels in the Holy Places. He even talked to the patriarch of Jerusalem and he promised him that a great army would come and rescue the Holy City. And the army must come out of France, sir. The Holy Father said so."

"The Holy Father can't leave Rome now and lead an army for two years, three. In that time the anti-pope, Ghibert, would be reigning in his place."

"The Holy Father wouldn't have to go, sir."

"Oh? Then who would lead the army?"

"You, Seigneur! I told Peter you'd lead it, if you only knew!"

Several people laughed. Godfrey's smile faded. Bennet watched him longingly. What if he would go—what if he could feel that a crusade to the Holy Land would make up for his action against the Pope? But before Godfrey could speak, gruff old Lancelot broke in.

"Peter is a fanatic! His ranting means no more than the cooing of the doves. Any man who would take up his cause would be as crazy as he!"

A rumble of agreement answered Lancelot. Lord Godfrey picked up a nut cake and broke it in two. But he did not eat it. He sat crumbling it into tiny bits.

"Step back," Laurent whispered, and Bennet gladly obeyed. He had done what Peter would have liked, spoken the message in the hall of a nobleman. Now all he could think about was that he was absolutely famished.

Managing to keep out of sight of the master of the pantry

and all the servers, Bennet ran to the scullery. The maid stood at the door, smiling shyly.

"Got anything to eat, Hughette?" the boy asked. It was the privilege of the scullery maid to save scraps to bring home, but Hughette was not greedy. Besides, since she was only twelve, the older maids took all the best leavings anyway.

She disappeared into the damp, sour place and in a moment was back with a roasted leg of rabbit. She held it out, smiling. Hughette was a dainty little thing in spite of her coarse, dirty apron. Her eyes were black, and her hair hung in black curls, but her skin was white as milk.

Bennet, hastily thanking her, grabbed the meat and streaked away. He didn't stop to eat until he came out on the bluff. The light had not yet faded from the river. It was a silver-smooth highway, seen from this lofty height, and it led, not into the depths of the Ardennes Forest, but straight to the hills of Jerusalem. Two riders traveled the highway on snow-white palfreys, a knight and a squire— Lord Godfrey of Bouillon, leader of the crusade, and his trusted squire, Bennet.

CHAPTER THREE
THE VOICE OF URBAN

The first yellow leaves of autumn were fluttering to the forest floor when Bennet met up with the troubadour. The fellow was making no secret of his coming. Even before he himself came in sight, his clear voice could be heard over the strumming of his lute. It was no surprise when the bend in the road disclosed a little gray donkey with a white face and the soft gray cross which, according to legend, all the donkeys have worn on their foreheads since the day one carried Christ into Jerusalem. His eyes were closed and his head down as if he might be finding his way by sniffing instead of seeing. The troubadour sat with one knee bent across the animal's back to accommodate the lute, the other foot in its purple shoe swinging against the goldenrod. He was not much older than Bennet, a dashing figure even though his purple and yellow had been rained on in the course of his journey and the white plume of his cap had been brushed by many an overhanging bough. When he saw the boy leaning against the beech tree, he kicked the little donkey gently to stop him.

"Well, where did you drop from?" he lilted as if this were part of the song.

"Bouillon Castle. May I ask the same of you, sir?"

"I never think of where I've been, only of where I'm going."

"And where are you going, sir?"

"Wherever the road leads."

"I'll show you the road that leads to my Lord Godfrey's castle. You'd be most welcome there."

"Undoubtedly so. I sing well, don't I?"

"Oh, very well, sir."

The young fellow laughed. His hair was black and curling, and his eyes were merry black, and when he smiled the dimples were deep in his smooth olive cheeks. Madame would be enchanted with this guest.

"You will come then, sir?" Bennet urged.

"With pleasure. But I'm not a sir. I'm Gareau. And my little donkey is Cuthbert. I named him after a bishop. Lead the way—what's your name?"

Bennet told him and he tangled the name into his song.

The boy leaped along the road. All summer he had haunted the forest, waylaying travelers with an invitation to partake of Lord Godfrey's hospitality. Not that he was

concerned for their welfare. But this was the only means
of bringing news of the crusade movement to Bouillon.
Everyone in the village and in the castle garrison talked
constantly about the splendid Army of God—all except
Lord Godfrey, who should be preparing to lead it. He
listened and said nothing. Bennet, naturally, could not speak
to the great lord. But he could see to it that there were
guests. And the main topic of interest was always the same:
the doings of Peter the Hermit.

Ku-ku Peter, riding on his bare-tailed mule, was rousing
France. How the crusade would be managed, who would
go and when, these were the questions asked over and over
while the candles burned lower in the sconces and the meat
juice congealed on the trenchers. The troubadour, Bennet
thought as he scurried toward the castle, might have some of
the answers. Troubadours were always welcome wherever
they went, both as carriers of news and singers of song. The
conversation would be lively in the Great Hall tonight!

Bennet was not disappointed. From his hidingplace in the
drapery he looked out proudly at this troubadour he had
found. Laurent had barely slipped his knife around one slice
of roast beef for Lord Godfrey before the conversation
turned to the crusade. Other squires carving before their
masters laid down their knives because the knights, listening, forgot to eat. The ladies' chattering fell silent. Gareau
alone held the floor.

"From the Alps to the Pyrenees and from the river Rhone
out to the blue Atlantic, a new spirit is moving through
France—light as the wind in the beeches, but it's there!
Old men who have spent their lifetime in hidden valleys
are wondering now what lies beyond the hills. Women who
have made but one journey, from their father's house to

their husband's, are thinking of how it would be to follow the long road to Jerusalem."

"Women? Surely not," a lady murmured, and the others echoed it excitedly.

"Of course women!" Gareau repeated. "Everyone must go. Peter has said so."

"Ah, Peter!"

"What of the hermit, old Ku-ku?" Lancelot asked.

"He's making the way clear for Urban."

Lord Godfrey started as if a nettle had suddenly pricked him. "Urban? He has decided to lead the crusade?"

"Not himself, Sire," Gareau answered, and his straight gaze met Godfrey's. "No. He will bring it together. Another will lead it."

Silence fell. Bennet, craning out from behind the chair, could see that Godfrey's knuckles were white with the strength of his grip on the carved arm.

"Every knight's sword is a holy thing, Sire," Gareau went on as if he spoke to Godfrey alone. "Within the hilt is a relic of some saint. The hilt itself is shaped like a cross. When the knight received the sword he promised to use it in defense of God. Now is the time!"

Still Godfrey did not reply. In his blue tunic with the silver light around his head and his face pale with emotion, he was like St. Michael not yet armed for conflict.

"The Holy Father is on his way over the Pyrenees now," the troubadour added. "By the end of October he will be at Cluny."

"Now there *is* a story!" Lancelot exclaimed. "The Pope doesn't travel unheralded, like a thief escaping from the sheriff. All of France would know if he were on his way!"

Gareau shrugged. "You will see, sir. The high lonely wastes of the Pyrenees would be the perfect place for an ambush. And Urban has many enemies led by Ghibert who claims the throne of Rome. His only safety lies in secrecy."

Lancelot laughed. But no one laughed with him.

And on the last day of October the proof came that Gareau was right. Out of the forest and up the long slope a rider came galloping on a dripping horse: the Holy Father had arrived at Cluny, the peaceful monastery he had left for the disquiet of Rome. He was calling an assembly of all the clergy in France as well as all the laity who might care to attend. The outward purpose was to enliven the priesthood into the spiritual leadership it had so nearly forgotten and to impress the lay people with their responsibility toward the Church.

But everyone knew what subject would take precedence: the Army of God for the march to Jerusalem.

The meeting was called for the middle of November at Clermont, two hundred miles to the south. There was very little time to prepare.

"The Holy Father doesn't want to allow time for sober thought," Gareau said when he heard the news. "Reap the harvest from the first spurt of enthusiasm, because once men are committed there will be no turning back, not with honor."

"Let's talk of going before we talk of turning back," Lord Godfrey said quickly. "Who will go with me to Clermont?"

"I will!" shouted every knight in the bailey.

The pages whispered excitedly, the dogs barked, and in the stables the great war chargers neighed as if they knew all the talk would result in something that concerned them.

"One squire to every knight, but no pages," Lord Godfrey decreed. "With men assembling from all over France, lodging and even food will be a problem. We'll have to restrict our numbers to those who could conceivably go on crusade."

There was disappointed murmuring among the pages. Leroy tossed his head as if he didn't care.

"So we don't go!" he said. "We'll hear all about it when they come back."

"I'm going," said Bennet. And then he wished he hadn't spoken. But Leroy only smiled at this piece of foolishness. There was no danger whatever that he would question Bennet about how he proposed to get to Clermont.

Bennet did have a plan. He was going to the conclave. He had to see Lord Godfrey's face when the Holy Father began to preach the crusade.

It was easy to keep his secret. Everyone was too busy preparing the knights for the long journey to wonder at the silence of one boy. So on the clear cold morning when Godfrey's party rode out of the Great Gate and down the long slope where the frost lay white as snow, Bennet also was ready. Watching from his hidingplace in the underbrush, he saw the palfreys step daintily on to the new white and leave a trampled brown trail behind them. They were making a trail into a new world. Lord Godfrey might be thinking the same thing, from the look of him. Attired in his finest blue silk, with a blue plume waving from his cap and silver sparkling at his belt, he sat straight and silent, his eyes on the forest ahead. All of his company followed his example, fifty knights in the blue livery of Bouillon, silent and straight in the saddle. They were not wearing armor, for the weight of it would slow the horses; but the silver spurs jingled and the silver discs fastened to the bridles hit against one another with a sound like little bells. The palfreys, caparisoned in silk as richly embroidered as their riders' cloaks, stepped high, necks proudly arched. Behind them on Cuthbert rode Gareau, his purple and yellow a bright contrast to all the blue.

Bennet waited until the gonfalon, a banner blue as the cold morning sky, disappeared into the autumn-yellow forest. Then he ran back to where he had left his palfrey tied to a tree. Quickly mounting, he turned her off at a right angle to the direction taken by Godfrey's company. He was going to parallel their route, reach the edge of the forest and then ride along the bank of the Meuse River until he came to the point where they must cross. He had done this with Old Barb once when they had pilfered horses for a day of adventuring, each taking a different route and meeting at the river. No one had found out about it, but Bennet hadn't dared do it again in spite of Barb's coaxing. He had shunned the old fellow since the poaching incident. But now the knowledge he had picked up from Old Barb was going to help him get to Clermont.

Bennet stopped only once to let his horse drink from a small stream. His anxiety lengthened the distance. Playing a game with Old Barb was quite different from racing against time. The gold of the trees had turned to gray in twilight when he finally came out on the bank of the Meuse. No other riders were in sight. He was wondering rather frantically whether to ride on or wait when the blue gonfalon of Bouillon appeared on the trail.

The knights glanced at first casually; then one shouted as he recognized the boy. Lord Godfrey was among the last to ride out of the forest and he joined the circle of knights with alarm.

"Is something the matter at the castle, boy?"

"No, Sire."

"Then what brings you here?"

"I want to go to Clermont with you, Sire."

"To Clermont!"

The knights echoed it, some laughing. Godfrey was exasperated.

"I can't let you come! Whatever made you play a trick like this?"

The boy had dismounted and he scuffed the dirt with his toe. He did not feel like a crusader now. He actually wondered himself why he had done this thing.

"Send him home!" old Lancelot thundered. "He has to learn to obey orders, and it was your order that only a picked company should come."

"He can't start back with darkness coming on," someone else said. "There are wolves in the forest."

Gareau urged Cuthbert out of the circle. "If I may speak, my lord? Let the boy go instead of me. I have no great compelling dream of seeing the Holy Father. He may have my place."

"Disobedience must not be rewarded!" Lancelot insisted.

But Lord Godfrey looked at Gareau as if he had just noticed that he was one of the party. "A great compelling dream, troubadour?"

"Yes, Sire. And all of France must be caught up in the same dream if the crusade is to be a success."

Lord Godfrey wheeled his horse, making the beautiful beast rear high. "Let him come! And you, too, Gareau. One more scrap of humanity will make no difference at Clermont. Ride on!"

And so when dawn broke across the rolling hills surrounding Clermont on the twenty-eighth day of November in 1095 —a day that would never be forgotten in history—Bennet was there.

The conferences had been going on for a week, by then, and each hour saw more people riding in on the roads leading from every quarter of France. The little town of Clermont itself, as well as all the neighboring villages up to an hour's ride away, had long been filled to overflowing. Later arrivals, Lord Godfrey among them, had to pitch tents and sling together shelters of brush on the wide fields and meadows, making another town with the banners of the knights and bannerets whipping in a gay display under the cold November sky. Yet even when the hoofprints of the horses froze into shallow cups and were filled with light dry snow no one seemed to mind the cold, for a marvelously penetrating warmth flowed out from the rambling old monastery which housed the Holy Father and his advisers.

Urban had not as yet appeared before the crowd, but news of the conferences came quickly and often. Three hundred bishops were in attendance and a great number of cardinals and archbishops, and with them the Pope was clearing away all the impediments which might hinder the great project of the Holy War. Private wars between nobles and families were forbidden and the Truce of God, confirming peace for the four days of Sunday through Wednesday of each week, was again asserted. Churches as well as the immediate area around roadside crucifixes were declared once more to be sanctuaries, and no one might pursue an adversary into such a refuge. Women, the clergy, merchants, and laborers, all those who would be left unprotected when the great army of fighting men would leave for the East, were to be given special guardianship. Every precaution was being taken to insure security at home so that no one would hesitate to leave his dependents and join the crusade.

"Our Pope from Cluny knows us well," Count Raymond of Toulouse said to Lord Godfrey. They were neighbors in the city of tents. "He would never get us off to the Holy Land if we had to leave our women and children, to say nothing of our lands, with a threat of civil war at home!"

Bennet, squatted around the corner of the tent out of sight, strained his ears for Lord Godfrey's reply. If one came, it was too quiet to be heard. Godfrey still listened and did not commit himself. Count Raymond was old, over fifty, and he had a long battle scar across his cheek and one eye was gone and his shoulders were bent and he had aches, he said, in all his bones; yet he talked constantly of the Great March. If only Lord Godfrey would do the same!

"Don't be concerned, there are many like him," Gareau said to Bennet in the privacy of the brush shelter they shared. "Why else is the Holy Father in France? If everyone was ready, there would be no need for him here. And remember, Lord Godfrey would not have come to Clermont if he had no interest in the idea."

Now at last the Holy Father would speak to the assembled people. In order that there would be less quarreling over places, each nobleman who had come with a large party had been assigned to a special area and his standard stuck in the ground. The dawn twilight was only breaking when Bennet, numb with cold, trotted through the forest of standards. Lord Godfrey's blue was up in front, well within hearing distance of the high platform from which the Holy Father would speak. Since yesterday the platform had been draped with the white and yellow of the papal flag, and there was an enormous chair like a throne. There were seats also for the other dignitaries who would speak before Urban, each chair draped with the colors of a noble house. Bennet shivered, but not alone with cold. This was how it would be in Jerusalem, color, excitement, gaiety among the squires and young knights assembling around the gonfalons; and instead of the winter-brown hills and half-bare trees there would be palms and sunshine and the glistening white temples Peter had told about. If there should be hardships on the way, who would mind when at the end of the journey there was Jerusalem, the golden city?

Long before the papal procession emerged from the monastery, the crowd had become so closely pressed that a few who fainted from excitement still remained standing upright. Bennet was as near as he could get to Lord Godfrey. The tall young nobleman did not take part in the chatter around him. His eyes were on the platform—as if he could hardly wait for his first glimpse of the Holy Father, Bennet decided. It was easy to know when the procession did emerge from the monastery because a low roar of acclaim began at that end of the throng and swept along like wind over a wheat field. Banners were caught up from their stakes and waved, everyone tried to stand on tiptoe but only those in front could see at all. From the descriptions they had heard through the week they knew what he looked like, the Vicar of Christ on earth—a handsome, commanding figure with hair and beard of yellow auburn and a manner of heavenly kindness. The fierce enmity of Ghibert had taught him forbearance, in exile he had learned patience. He was a saint, this Urban who had been the humble monk of Cluny.

Yet Urban did not lead the procession onto the platform. The first figure was a thin scarecrow of a man. Carrying his rude cross, his rough brown robe dirtier than ever and his hair and beard in a tangled mat, he clambered up the steps.

"Ku-ku Peter!" Bennet exclaimed.

"Is *that* the hermit?" Lord Godfrey asked incredulously. "I thought he'd be——"

What Lord Godfrey thought was lost in the general clamor, for now Urban had ascended into view. He was all in white with a long cloak that flowed out into a train, and there was about him the simplicity of a man who did not need splendid dress to draw attention to his greatness. In tribute, the crowd fell silent. They would have knelt but there was no room. Caps came off until only the heads of the few women in the crowd remained covered. Bennet, warm though he was from the bodies around him, shivered again. One after another the princes of the church took their places in the chairs, each more resplendent than the last, cardinals in red, bishops in purple and green, and all the glowing color heightened by the plain black and brown of of a few monks.

The Holy Father was barely seated in the great chair when Ku-ku Peter stepped forward and at once began to speak.

"My brothers, you have not come to hear me. The good Father of us all has a message far more important than mine. But because I have seen the things you have not seen, and because in the Holy Place I had a vision of Jesus Christ Himself weeping for His city, our Father has asked that I speak first and tell you of these things."

For nearly an hour Peter described his journey to Jerusalem. His voice broke with emotion when he spoke of the Holy Sepulchre, tears ran down his face. When finally he crumpled into a ragged heap on the edge of the platform, men were weeping with him. Lord Godfrey, Bennet saw, was pale and his jaw set. Beyond him Count Raymond mopped his one eye.

The Holy Father rose then, his golden staff in his hand and all the white draperies flowing out behind him. He spoke very quietly.

"Dear brothers in Christ, I come to you in a great crisis. I know you to be true servants of God, my kinsmen and countrymen, and He will not find us wanting. As He has cared for you, so you will care for His children who cry out for help. The cry is loud and pitiful, my brothers. Alexius Comnenus, Emperor of the East, has sent messengers imploring our aid. If we close our ears, we and our children will be cast into outer darkness to endure the vengeance of God!"

How long Urban spoke no one knew exactly, for the spell he cast over his audience was too profound to be reckoned in time. He had not seen Jerusalem in the hands of the infidels as Peter had, yet he carried his hearers there with him.

"Our God who became man for our redemption passed His earthly life in that chosen land. Palestine is our inheritance, Jerusalem is our treasure. Yet this dwelling place of Jesus Christ, the cradle of our salvation, is no longer sacred! Christ expelled the buyers and sellers from the temple but now from its sanctuary the doctrine of the devil is openly preached. Beasts of burden stand in the temple yards, the faithful are slain. How can we live and not put an end to such an evil?" Urban moved to the edge of the platform and his full-toned voice touched the very summits of the hills where the donkeys grazed. "To every man, woman, and child who will make the solemn crusade to the Holy Land, I now grant a plenary indulgence at the hour of death! Blessed are they who will march in the mighty army of the Lord, for to them will be given life eternal!"

Urban paused, and a great shout broke forth from the assembled multitude.

"It is the will of God!"

The people swayed together, arms uplifted toward heaven, tears running down their faces, in ecstasy as if already they beheld the beatific vision. But when the white Pope held up his hands, they were quiet in a single breath.

"You will go," he said gently, and the gentleness carried farther than the thundering, beyond the crests of the hills where the donkeys raised their heads to listen. "Go on your errand of love for the faithful who cannot defend themselves, of love which will put out of sight all the ties which bind you to home. Your home is not here. All the world is exile, and all the world is at the same time your country. 'It is the will of God,' let that be your war cry when you unsheath your swords against the enemy. You are soldiers of the cross. Wear then on your breasts the blood-red sign of Him who died for the salvation of your souls! Wear it as a token of His help which will never fail you! Wear it as the pledge of a vow which can never be recalled!"

With both arms outstretched as if he were nailed to a cross, Urban made his plea. Suddenly on the long stairs to the platform appeared knights in bright silver mail. Each carried an enormous silver tray, and on the trays lay mounds of red cloth.

"There are your crosses!" Urban cried. "Who will be the first crusader?"

"I, Your Holiness!" someone replied in a ringing voice, and a bishop who stood a head taller than those around him began to push his way forward.

"Bishop Adhemar of Puy!" Count Raymond exclaimed. "If I cannot be first, then he should be."

The bishop was now on the platform and kneeling before Urban who took from a tray a bright red cross cut out of cloth. Laying it over Adhemar's heart, he blessed him.

"You, Adhemar of Puy, will be my spiritual leader of the crusade. In you will be vested the powers and dignity of the papal legate, and may God bless you." The Pope turned to the crowd. "Repeat the confiteor and I will give you the general absolution before you take the sacred symbol."

The prayer roared from hill to hill; then Urban's hand made the sign of the cross.

If a spur was needed to urge hands to reach for the red crosses, the sight of the symbol on the breast of the famed bishop was enough. Other bishops surged forward with priests and monks after them. Count Raymond charged into the ranks as if they were Turks to be vanquished.

But Lord Godfrey stood still. Rivers of men parted around him, jostling and shoving. Bennet watched with dying hope while the silk shoulders of the noblemen gave way to the rough wool of their servants. Lord Godfrey had let his opportunity pass, for he would not go forward with the cooks and grooms. Sadly Bennet left the field. From the top of the hill he looked back. The Master of Bouillon still remained under the blue gonfalon, one hand holding the staff and the silk folds touching his bowed head.

Night came, colder than the day and with a slight mist. Bennet had spent the intervening hours wandering disconsolately by himself. Beside a stream where deep red dogwood grew in long graceful stems, he flung himself down. Why Lord Godfrey would not take the cross with the others was something he did not know. Perhaps it was some worrisome reason left over from the Roman campaign. To see the cross taken by Count Raymond and every nobleman and knight, that was a bitter sight when Lord Godfrey was not among them. The boy pulled a couple of twigs from the dogwood and tied them with a strip of bark into a rude cross. Now he had a cross. Like Peter's.

Gareau was snoring in the little brush shelter when Bennet came back. Everyone else, from the sounds, was asleep in the tents and shelters. Except one person. A tall, cloaked figure advanced.

"You were disappointed, weren't you, boy, when I didn't

go forward to take the cross with the others?" Lord Godfrey asked.

"Yes, Seigneur."

"But if I'm not worthy, Bennet—what then?"

"*You* not worthy, my lord?"

Godfrey shook his head and the hood of the cloak fell. Now Bennet could see his face plainly. His cheeks appeared sunken, his eyes deep in his skull.

"King Henry called for an army and I brought together my knights and we marched to Rome. I thought our cause was right. But now I know Henry was acting at the request of our own King Philip, and Philip was angry because the Holy Father would not give him permission to put his wife away and marry another. I sinned greatly, taking up arms against Rome. Our good Pope Urban could not forgive me."

"Couldn't you ask him, Sire?"

Lord Godfrey was startled. He smiled, then laughed aloud.

"The simple logic of the young! Of course, why not ask him?"

He grasped the boy's hand, felt the tiny wooden crucifix Bennet still carried and opened his fingers.

"What have you here, boy?"

"Nothing, Sire. I made it this afternoon."

"Red. A red cross. Will you give it to me, Bennet?"

"Of course, my lord, if you want it."

Godfrey closed his hand over the rude little cross. Then he put his arm tightly around Bennet's shoulders.

"Thank you, son. Sleep now. We'll be starting for home early in the morning."

"Yes, Seigneur."

Bennet, wanting to laugh and shout and leap higher than the gonfalons, saw Lord Godfrey hurry away with the step of a man who knows his errand and must accomplish it immediately. He was on his way to seek an audience with the Holy Father. Urban should know all about forgiveness. Only he could open the road to the Holy Land for Lord Godfrey of Bouillon.

CHAPTER FOUR
THE RED CROSS OF CRUSADE

On Christmas morning, a month after the return from
Clermont, Lord Godfrey and all his household and garrison
took the red cross of crusade. Everyone had been mystified
at the change in the duke. What had happened, they asked,
on that last night at Clermont? Bennet knew, but he told
no one. Since that intimate moment on the foggy hillside,
the boy had watched the preparations from a distance.
Many details fell to Lord Godfrey. He had to raise money
to equip and support his army, decide who should be in-

cluded from among the hundreds who instantly made known their desire to march under his banner, study routes and make plans which might span two years or more. Bennet, hopeful that perhaps in some way he might become a squire, set about a rigorous program of training. He lifted weights, climbed ropes let down from the castle wall, danced in an armored shirt whenever he could borrow one from under his father's watchful eye. A squire had to be physically ready for any exertion. He would be responsible for his master's weapons and must carry the heavy lances for long hours. He would go unarmed to the battlefield where he must not take part in the fray, but squires had been known to rush in and, snatching a weapon, save their masters' lives. Bennet could do that. He didn't even have to shut his eyes to see himself rescuing Lord Godfrey on the sands of Palestine.

He spent a great deal of time praying, and on the morning that dawned into Christmas he was weary because he had spent the whole night kneeling in the chapel. Laurent had kept the vigil also. He had been Lord Godfrey's body squire for two years, and now he was sixteen and ready to receive the accolade. Laurent had not dozed at all, but it had been difficult for Bennet to keep awake. In the first fifteen minutes he had run through all the anxious things he had to say to the Lord in the Blessed Sacrament. After that there didn't seem to be much to think about except that he must get to the Holy Land. He awoke with a start when the Mass began.

The Mass and the knighting ceremony were long. By the time Duke Godfrey knelt before the altar to receive the first of the red crosses, the winter sun was streaming through the high windows and he looked more than ever like St. Michael. After him came Laurent in his bright new chain mail, for this young knight would be the standard-bearer, and then the knights in order of their age and service. At the end came every able-bodied man in Bouillon—the tanners, blacksmiths, cooks and bakers, the marshals, the masters of the pantry and kitchen—everyone but Josef, the chief armorer. Bennet had known his father would not be among the number; yet when he saw the bent figure remain kneeling where others must step around him, he was so ashamed that he couldn't remain in the chapel.

Lurching over feet, Bennet made his way out. Someone was in the hall very close to the door, listening. It was Hughette. Her smile was bright and she spoke in a joyful whisper.

"Bennet, did you see him?"

"See who?"

"My father! He's going on crusade with Lord Godfrey! And he's taking all of us with him!"

"Girls can't go."

"We can if there's someone to take care of us. And my mother and father will both be there. Oh, Bennet, if only you were going!"

"I'd rather stay home," Bennet said gruffly.

Hughette's dark eyes widened and her smile died. "Poor Bennet," she said gently. "We're not going until spring. Maybe by then——"

But the boy heard no more. Running swiftly, he slammed into a cook who had left the chapel early to see to the soup, picked himself up and raced along the small corridor to the door opening at the river bluff, out and down the long path to the village. He burst into his own home so abruptly that his mother, bent over a steaming kettle in the fireplace, slopped the porridge. The children playing on the hearth looked up in expectant silence, fingers in their mouths.

"What is it, son?" Violette asked quickly. "What has happened?"

"Nothing, Mama."

"So you make me burn my hand for nothing! Shut the door behind you."

The boy gave the door a kick and flung himself down on the bench beside the table. Breaking a chunk from the black loaf, he crammed it into his mouth. Choking himself on the bread helped somehow to work off his wrath.

"Mama, everybody's going!" he cried when he could swallow. "Hughette's whole family—everybody but us! My father is the only man in Bouillon without the courage to go to Jerusalem! *My own father!*"

A cold wind blew around Bennet's feet. He saw his mother stiffen, the children grow wide-eyed. He knew what it was—his father had come in. He hadn't swung the door quite shut and Josef had heard every word he said.

"Close the door, Antoine," Josef said. He came around the table. Bennet rose, his knees hard against the bench behind him. Papa did not punish his children often, but when he did they never forgot it. And disrespect was something he would not tolerate. His face always had a waxen look from working inside, but now he was deathly white and his eyes burned dark in the deep sockets. His hair, neat enough in the chapel, had blown on end and it bristled like his beard.

"Sit down," he ordered, and waited until the boy obeyed. "I should whip you for calling me a coward. You ought to know me better. But in this fever that has taken hold of France, many sons will be saying the same of their fathers. All they see is the golden dream of Jerusalem at the end of a journey that is like a picnic on a summer day, everybody is happy, the new kingdom is paradise. What they do not consider is that for many it will be a journey to the grave.

And the women and children will fall in the greatest numbers. Would you want your mother, your young brothers and sisters, to lie in unmarked graves in a heathen land?"

"Hughette's father isn't afraid," Bennet mumbled.

Never in his life had he dared speak so to his father. For a moment he thought Josef would strike him. But the fists opened to lie flat on the table and the old man sat down as if he were very weary.

"Listen to me, son. Hughette's father is tired of being a tanner. If he stays in Bouillon he will go on being a tanner for the rest of his life, but on crusade he will be something different, a brave man going into foreign lands to conquer for the Lord. He may turn out to be a great hero, because a man's worth will lie in how well he can stand cold and heat and hunger and thirst, and the peasants will do better than the noblemen for they know all about misery. Thousands of people will go like that, wanting to escape out of what they are into what they wish they were."

"Not Lord Godfrey, Papa!" Bennet protested.

"No, Lord Godfrey has a different reason, to do penance for his sin against Rome. He wants to be able to live with himself again."

"He's a noble knight!"

"Of course! And so are Count Raymond and Robert Short Breeches, and Godfrey's brother, Baldwin. Baldwin's a noble knight! He wants a whole new kingdom for himself!"

"Tancred doesn't want anything for himself, Papa."

Josef's face softened. "No, you are right, Bennet. Tancred is the youngest of all the knights and he has the purest motive, simply to save the Holy Land. But a boy of seventeen, who follows him? Other boys!"

Bennet felt an inner glow, for this was the way Papa talked with the smiths in the armory, man to man.

"Oh, for the one who goes because he loves God, there will be fifty—a hundred—others who want something for themselves. Take the plenary indulgence promised by the Holy Father to every crusader, it's a good thing in itself but now all kinds of crimes will be committed because at the hour of death what happens? All sin is forgiven and we gain heaven!"

"To listen to you, one would think the Church is bribing an army to go to Palestine!" Violette declared, although it was seldom she spoke up to her husband.

"The Holy Father knows men," Josef said. "And understand this, Bennet. The Holy Land is in desperate need of help, but the help of fighting *men*, not women and children. I'm too old to go, I'd die on the way. And as for going thousands of miles to seek God, why should I do that when I can find Him on the altar of Bouillon?"

"Papa, you'd let me go on crusade with Lord Godfrey, wouldn't you?" Bennet asked.

"You will not lie in a foreign grave!" Violette exclaimed.

But Josef looked at her with a smile. "Wife, we can safely say that if Lord Godfrey wants him, he may go. Give us some porridge."

The answer stung. One minute Josef talked to his son man to man, the next he spoke of him indulgently as if he were a child. Bennet jumped up in fury and the bench whacked over behind him. He slapped the table with the flat of his hand.

"I'm going to Jerusalem, Papa! If Lord Godfrey doesn't want me, then I'll run away and go with somebody else! Because I'm going, Papa, and nobody can stop me! I'm going to be knighted in the Church of the Holy Sepulchre!"

He whirled and ran out of the house. He didn't quite know how he had ever dared to speak like that to his father.

But the new spirit of crusade was like a yeast foaming over, not to be held down by any of the old respects or conventions. All over France it was the same. Zeal for the crusade flared out as defiance and everyone contended against old ties for the privilege of going. Sons defied their fathers, husbands ordered reluctant wives to get on with the spinning and weaving so there would be new clothes for the journey. Monks came out of their monasteries where the routine that had appeared to be the road to heaven was suddenly a dull rut. Criminals were demanding and getting release from prison to join the army, peasants were being forgiven their debts because no one must go with a worry to distract him on the way. The crops had failed the summer before and famine had been feared for the winter months, but suddenly there was plenty. Wealthy nobles who had hoarded up grain for a better market decided to sell because they needed money for equipment. Land became ridiculously cheap, arms and horses went up in price. Because there was so much buying and selling, people said that already good had come to France, and the cause of the crusade became more popular than ever.

The winter days rolled into weeks and spring came again to the Ardennes Forest. Still Lord Godfrey had not appointed a squire to take Laurent's place. Bennet, stubbornly maintaining to his father that he was going to the Holy Land, went on with his rigorous physical feats. On an afternoon in early April he was working at the most difficult of all, a climb up the thirty-foot castle wall. The groove had been built specially for the purpose, its two perpendicular sides from four to five feet apart. There was no foothold except the stones already smoothed by many climbers. The only means of ascent was by the pressure of his arms and legs.

Bennet climbed facing the wall. It was a little easier that way, not seeing the ground falling farther away below. His muscles ached and his breathing hurt, but he was nearly to the top when he heard a hail from below. Leroy, of course. Nobody else would take a chance on startling a climber so far up. Bennet made no reply until he gained the top and swung himself to a seat on the wall. Leroy, brilliantly clean in his blue livery, stood below. He had not tried to scale the wall yet. That was a performance required only of squires.

"Lord Godfrey wants to see you!" Leroy called. "Right away!"

Bennet took several long breaths. This could hardly be a trick. And yet there was no reason why the duke should squander even a precious minute on him. If he had done something wrong it would be Edmond, the marshal, who would send for him, not Lord Godfrey.

The easiest way down was to run along the wall to the stairs and then descend into the bailey, but Bennet let himself slide in between the perpendicular stones again. He knew he was showing off. If he should lose his footing, Leroy would be pleased. Faster than was prudent, he lurched his way down and jumped the last few feet.

Leroy pretended not to be impressed. "Lord Godfrey has just made me his esquire of honor, his body squire," he said. "I knew he would. My uncle, the Duke of Normandy, is his friend."

Bennet's teeth bit hard together. "Why does he want to see me?"

"He didn't say. Go to the rock chamber. You'll find him there."

Bennet would have liked, for once, to wash his face and comb his hair, but he couldn't keep the duke waiting. He ran straight to the little chamber and stood at attention in the doorway.

Of late, Lord Godfrey had spent a great deal of time in the little place hewn out of solid rock. Now he sat on the ledge where his grandfather had sat to look out through the natural crack in the rock and see the enemy storming up the long slope to the castle. It was an impregnable cell, lighted only by skyshine through the crack. Here, in quiet hours, the Master of Bouillon planned his journey to the Holy Land.

"Come in, Bennet," he said. All traces of illness and anxiety were gone from him now. He had taken to training again with his knights, and his arms, bare to the shoulder, were smooth muscle. Bennet tried not to squirm under that calm inspection. If only he knew what Lord Godfrey had in mind. . . .

"You know, of course, that I have taken a long time about choosing a squire," the duke said finally. "If I were staying at home, it would not be so important. But on crusade, my life may at times depend on the courage and faithfulness of my squire. I must be certain he is absolutely trustworthy."

"Leroy is trustworthy, Sire," Bennet said. That was true. Whatever belonged to Leroy—his palfrey, his saddle, even his master—was his to defend stoutly.

Godfrey nodded. "Everyone tells me so. If I didn't believe that, I would never take him on our journey." He paused, measuring Bennet again with his clear gray eyes; and then, unexpectedly, he smiled. "Yes, I'm right about you, too. I want you with me. I know how you've been training yourself all winter for the physical requirements of a knight, and I know how you've hoped and prayed—and never given up. There's no reason why your humble birth should deny you what you want and deserve. Many of the leaders will be picking men for their worth rather than the accident of nobility." Lord Godfrey stood up and laid his hand on the boy's shoulder. "You have the great, compelling dream, Bennet. I'll make you my stable squire. You'll come with me to Palestine."

Bennet didn't know how long he stood there, staring up at Lord Godfrey, trying to believe that he really had heard the magic words. At last he found his voice.

"Thank you, Sire! I'll never desert you! I'll always be there with your charger, and your armor. . . . Thank you, my lord!"

"Will you try to get along better with Leroy?"

"Oh, yes, Sire!"

Godfrey laughed. "Very well. Now run and tell the good news to your father."

Through the old castle halls Bennet sped to the armory. Josef was seated on a table with his foot tucked under him, his grizzled head bent over the chain armor he was oiling. The boy flung himself against the table, nearly rolling over the gourd of oil.

"Papa! Papa, you said if Lord Godfrey would take me, I could go to Palestine! Remember?"

Josef's hand was still. "I remember."

"I can go! I'm to be his stable squire! And you know what it means to be a squire, Papa—someday I can be a knight!" Bennet stood up very tall and straight. "Papa, now I *will* be knighted by Lord Godfrey in the Church of the Holy Sepulchre! In Jerusalem!"

Josef looked long at his son. Then he raised his hand, oily from the rag, and laid it on the boy's head.

"Go, my son, with my blessing," he said. "And may God go with you all!"

Long years later, when Bennet thought of his father, it

was this picture of him which came to mind—the patient, bent figure with the gnarled hands working away at the links which would defend some knight in his journey to the Holy Land.

In a ceremony which was actually a part of the knighting ritual, Bennet and Leroy with a dozen others received the hauberk of chain mail from Lord Godfrey. This would be their sole defense in case of attack. The helmet and lance and breastplate would not be theirs until they won the spurs of knighthood. Bennet was so proud of his new mail that he slept in it the first few nights and awoke in the morning to feel deep, sore grooves in his shoulders and side. If Godfrey wanted devotion, he had it now. Long before Leroy stirred on his pallet outside the master's door, Bennet was up and carrying warm water for washing. Then he waited while Leroy laid out the duke's clothes and helped him to dress. After Mass he ran to the stable to see that the favorite palfrey was ready, to the armory to polish the lances or rub a little extra oil on the chain mail. If Godfrey went hunting, he rode behind him and carried the hooded falcon on his wrist. He worked so hard that he grew thin, and his mother was worried about him; but his father spoke very crossly to cover his pride in his son.

"Forget him now, he's a man, a crusader! Come the middle of this month of April, we'll never see him again."

By the middle of April, however, the only one who appeared to be ready for departure was Old Barb. All winter he had been stealing what he needed, although he could have had the things for the asking—boiled leather for sandals to protect his feet from the burning sands, a goatskin with the hair still on it, a length of linen from which he made himself another shirt and a purse. And then one night he disappeared. A horse also was missing from the stable, and his wild dogs were gone from the cave. Old Barb, everyone said, had joined Peter the Hermit, but no one knew for sure.

In June reports of Peter's march came back to Bouillon. The rabble of released prisoners, cutthroats, and brigands, several thousand strong, had reached Cologne in Germany. Robbing and begging because they had no supplies of their own, the mob fought among themselves while Walter the Penniless and Ku-ku Peter quarreled over who should be the leader. No agreement being reached, three thousand elected to follow Walter and the rest surged after Peter. They had only reached the borders of Hungary when a third horde streamed together after the banner of Emico, Count of Leiningen, and a fourth under the leadership of a monk named Gottschalk.

"And there is still another band," said Gareau, who had brought this news. "A crazy gang has come together to be led by a goose and a goat——"

A shout of derision interrupted him, for he was telling his story in the Great Hall before all the knights.

"A goose and a goat," Gareau insisted. "Laugh if you like, but the people are ignorant enough to believe that these things are entered into by the Holy Ghost. And so with such leaders they can do no wrong, and they are so feared that the people of Hungary are throwing themselves into rivers or wells to escape when they hear they're coming!"

Godfrey leaped to his feet and began to stride up and down before his table. The dogs slunk out of his way.

"We'll have to start our march! If we delay longer, there will be such sentiment against all crusaders that we'll be attacked on sight!"

"It's getting the riffraff out of the way, my lord," Gareau said. "There will be few to demand passage with your army."

"True. Still, I'm going to start in August. If Count Raymond is not ready, he can choose his own time. Tancred is already in Italy. My brothers Eustace and Baldwin will come with me. The fifteenth of August, the Assumption of Our Lady! That will be our date!"

On the fifteenth of August, in summer sun with arms aglitter and the blue gonfalon of Bouillon standing out in the breeze beside the purple standard of Lorraine, Lord Godfrey rode forth at the head of his army of crusaders. The knights wore shining armor, silver medallions shot back the sun from the bridles of the palfreys, spurs jingled, and lances made a brightly speared forest above the helmeted heads. Beside each knight rode his squire, bareheaded, a scarf of the master's color fluttering around his throat and his new hauberk oiled to the glow of silver. Sometimes the squire carried his knight's shield with a painted design of a dragon or angel or some other symbol. Usually he led the great war charger his master would ride into battle, for these knights had only one squire. The chargers frisked like heavy-footed colts. They alone carried empty saddles since all their great strength must be saved for combat. After the knights came the foot soldiers clothed in leather, on their left arms the long shields to protect them from enemy arrows and on their heads the helmets which made them look like thousands of beetles pouring down the slope. The soldiers carried a variety of weapons—swords, heavy clubs, slings from which could be thrown stones and balls of lead, bows and crossbows and knives. If it were not for the soldiers, it would almost seem that the entire Duchy of Lorraine was going on a picnic.

In the rear, behind the foot soldiers, rumbled the awkward carts drawn by oxen and filled with supplies and precious things that could not be left behind. On top of one rode an old lady with her spinning wheel, on another a cat purred contentedly with a litter of kittens. Whole families of peasants walked beside their carts, the children asking how long it would be before they would get to Jerusalem, the old and the young calling good-bys as if they would be back at sunset.

At the head of the garrison immediately behind Lord Godfrey and Leroy rode Bennet, his livery new and clean, his hauberk shining, his curly head high as he held tight to the rein of the prancing war charger he was leading. He kept his eyes straight ahead upon the blue gonfalon Laurent held so steady because he did not want to see Mama and Papa waving for the last time. They might not be here when he returned with the palms from Jerusalem.

"The will of God!" the warriors cried. "It is the will of God!"

The big war horns that were the oliphants blasted a long farewell.

Many times on the way Bennet would hear that cry and the call of oliphants in both victory and defeat, but never with quite the loneliness of this final salute as the army moved deep into the Ardennes Forest.

CHAPTER FIVE
ON THE MARCH

As the long line of march wound through the Ardennes, other families and soldiers joined it, and by the time Godfrey reached the Rhine River, which was his assembly point, his followers numbered forty thousand. With him were his brothers Baldwin and Eustace and their own smaller armies. Baldwin had been destined for the priesthood by his father and had already taken minor orders when the call to crusade came along. Thankfully he left the monastery, for the life had never appealed to him; and since he had a wide acquaintance among the clergy his company included a number of priests and nuns. Baldwin and Eustace both were tall and strong like Godfrey, with the same light brown hair and gray eyes. But Baldwin had no patience and the men behind his red standard would jump when he roared, and Eustace was a shadow of Godfrey, always waiting to follow his brother's lead. Robert of Normandy, the son of William the Conqueror, was already waiting at the Rhine, red-faced and bleary-eyed from too much sampling of the wine, cheerful and loudly devoted to Godfrey. Robert, Count of Flanders, named the Lance of the Christians by his followers, headed a band of Flemish peasants whose stout legs and childlike faith would make them good travelers. With him was the wealthiest of the leaders, Stephen, Count of Chartres, Troyes, and Blois, who owned a castle for every day in the year and spent his nights in his tent writing letters to the beautiful wife he had left at home. The other princes would take different routes and all would meet at Constantinople: Hugh the Great, who was the brother of the King of France, old one-eyed Raymond of Toulouse, young Tancred who had wanted to be a monk, and his uncle, Bohemund, the boisterous ruler of Tarentum in Italy. Half the world, it seemed, would be on the march to the Holy Land from Constantinople.

There was food in plenty for the passage through Germany and the march was uneventful, the knights said. To Bennet it was all so different that he felt like asking with the children, "Is this Jerusalem?" each time they approached a new town. People spoke in a strange tongue, their dress and their houses and even their dogs were different. But their look of wariness and even hostility became familiar. Peter's host had swarmed through here and plundered these very towns, and the people had no reason to believe that Godfrey's army would be any better. But as the gleaming knights passed by, then the foot soldiers and the archers, and there was no attack, there were even a few shy smiles when the French children waved to the Germans. And so Godfrey reached the frontier town of Tollenburg unmolested and made camp for the last time before entering Hungary.

It was here that they heard the first real news of the armies that had preceded them. Gareau on his donkey, a part of the army and yet unattached to it, had formed the habit of riding ahead and around the outriders, picking up news and information. Bennet was seated on the grass near his master's tent when Cuthbert trotted up the slight rise. Godfrey had taken off his armor and the leather shirt that went under it, and in the cool of the evening he wore only linen as he sat at the table before his tent.

"Where have you been, troubadour?" he called.

Gareau threw himself down on the carpet at Godfrey's feet. "In the market yonder," he said, waving toward the steeples and turrets of the town. "There's talk of nothing but the crusaders. Hear what's become of them, Sire!"

Walter the Penniless had crossed Hungary with little trouble, having taken the same route followed by Godfrey. But when they came into Bulgaria, his riotous horde found that the governor of Belgrade had closed all the markets, and so the plundering began. There was a fierce hand-to-fist battle in which Walter himself escaped and with a few hundred followers went on to Constantinople. Peter the Hermit, coming along a little later, met the same reception in Bulgaria. At the town of Semlin on the Bulgarian border he was nearly destroyed.

"Somebody warned Peter that the Hungarians under their hunchback king, Kalmany, were going to attack him on the land side while the Bulgarian forces swarmed over the river," Gareau ended. "When clothing which was known to have belonged to Walter's people was waved over the wall of Semlin, Peter couldn't hold back his wild mob. They broke into the town and murdered everybody. Then the Hungarians came up and drove them on to the river bridge and the bridge broke and . . . well, Peter has reached Constantinople with perhaps a hundred of the followers who set out with him."

Bennet saw how Leroy's hand trembled so that he must set down the wine cup. He too was trembling. This did not sound like a picnic. Lancelot and Laurent and some of the other knights had drawn around to listen, and their faces were as tense as Godfrey's.

"What of the others, the monk Gottschalk and those deluded ones who followed the goose and the goat?" Godfrey asked.

"All slaughtered, my lord. By the Hungarians."

"But there were hundreds of them!"

No one replied. Between the town and the camp ran the Leitha River, smooth as the Semois at home. On the other side lay the domain of the hunchback king who had already been tried too far. And now another horde—lawless, so far as he would know—were knocking at his door.

"We'll give him a hostage to keep until we are safely across Hungary," Godfrey said at last. "Then Kalmany will know we mean to keep our promise of peace, because if our army should misbehave we know he would kill our hostage. I'll go myself, perhaps."

"No, Sire!" Lancelot thundered. "Either of your brothers, but not you! Kalmany wouldn't expect it!"

"Bennet, run and fetch my brothers, Eustace and Baldwin," Godfrey said with his eyes still fixed on the deceptively quiet town across the river.

Baldwin, when he heard that he was to be the hostage, roared his unwillingness, but in the end he went with his family and servants to the hunchback's camp, and the army passed calmly through Hungary. At the far border a stop was made while Baldwin rejoined the company.

"I'm through playing the mouse!" he declared angrily. "If the governor of Belgrade wants a hostage, somebody else will have to go!"

But none was required. The army, with its reputation for peaceful buying of supplies, was permitted to continue through Bulgaria without trouble. Down the Morava River, through the swelling green mountains along the Nisava River they went, leaving winter behind. The crusade, everyone said, was going to meet with no hindrance at all. Lord Godfrey's policy of fairness would open the way clear to Jerusalem.

And then they came to Philippopolis. There a messenger was waiting with grim news. Hugh the Great, impetuously rushing on ahead, had been captured by Alexius, Emperor of the East, and was being held prisoner at Constantinople.

"Alexius asked for help from the West!" Godfrey exclaimed. "What is he thinking of, to imprison the brother of the King of France? I don't believe it!"

"I do," said Baldwin.

Godfrey whirled on him. "Why?"

"Because he's afraid."

"Afraid of *us*, his allies?"

Baldwin sat down beside the table, for the blue tent seemed crowded with the big men. Bennet, crouched on the ground outside where he could peek through a crack, saw the earnest faces against the canopy as if they were warrior angels hovering in space.

"I've never seen Alexius, but I can read his mind," Baldwin explained. "Look at what he has done. We know that he's slowly losing his own empire of Byzantium to the invading Turks, and he must have aid immediately. But if he sent messages to the West urging us to come and save his empire, would we do it? Of course not. We have no interest in him. So he appeals to us as Christians, come and save the Holy Land from the infidel, rescue Constantinople because it too is a sacred place! It happens to be his capital city, also, but he doesn't mention that." Baldwin looked around with a rueful smile. "And we swallowed the bait. We're here."

Godfrey, standing tall beside his brother, had listened intently. "Very well, Baldwin, I grant that Alexius is thinking first of himself. But the fact remains that Jerusalem is in the hands of the Turks, who desecrate the Holy Places, and if we don't heed the Holy Father's call to free the city from the infidels, then we don't deserve the name of Christians!"

"And Alexius is merely a stumbling block on our way," said Eustace.

"You haven't told us, Baldwin, why this crafty Greek has imprisoned Hugh," Robert of Flanders remarked. "How could he be afraid of us?"

"Because we are arriving in such numbers," Baldwin answered promptly. "Constantinople is our meeting place for all the leaders before we cross over into Asia Minor, so naturally there will be huge armies right under Alexius' windows. And if we should change our minds about being so friendly, and decide to take Constantinople for ourselves, who could stop us? Not the emperor! We'd outnumber his forces two or three to one."

"That's no excuse for throwing Hugh into prison!" Eustace declared.

"The fact remains that he's there," said Robert of Flanders. "How are we going to get him out?"

"Without declaring war on the emperor," said Godfrey. "That's our problem."

The candle burned long in the tent that night while Godfrey and his brothers interrupted one another in their hurry to solve the problem of Hugh, and Robert of Normandy shouted to let Hugh take care of himself and old Lancelot muttered that they all should have stayed at home. The conference broke up when the first light touched the wavelets of the Marica River and a trusted knight rode off as ambassador with a party of ten to demand the immediate release of Hugh.

The messengers traveled swiftly, and within a week they were back with curious news. Hugh was being entertained as a royal guest, not held prisoner, Alexius had told the ambassador. Furthermore, he had added with many smiles, Hugh's great weariness from the long journey made it impossible for him to receive visitors. In the crossing from Italy he had been shipwrecked and that ordeal, along with the overland trip from the Dalmatian coast, had tired him to the point of exhaustion. He must not be disturbed.

"So you didn't see Hugh at all?" Godfrey asked.

"No, Sire," the knight replied. "But he managed to get a message to us. He begs you to bring about his release immediately. It won't be easy, for the emperor is scared right to his fat heart. He hears of all the armies descending on Constantinople and he feels he is in worse danger from us than from his old enemies, the Seljukian Turks. So he is detaining Hugh as a hostage, nothing less."

Godfrey never swore, but he leaped up and strode out of the blue tent as if he must have new air to breathe. Bennet was barely in time to hold aside the flap. Baldwin and Eustace, Lancelot and Laurent followed him out and together they stood looking down on the long river that would lead them finally to Constantinople.

"Soon Tancred will be joining us, and a little later Raymond of Toulouse," Godfrey said. "We are the outriders of the whole crusading army and it is up to us to clear the way. Apparently Alexius has forgotten that for two years he has been sending cries of help to the West. Now that help is coming, he treats us like enemies!"

"Could we change the meeting place, Sire?" Laurent asked. "Go into Asia by some other route?"

"No!" Godfrey said curtly. "We have to hire boats for passage, and the shortest water route is from Constantinople across to Krysopolis. I've heard you can look across into Asia Minor. If Alexius will not let us gather peaceably, we'll give him a taste of something else. In the morning we resume our march!"

Bennet, listening, shivered. He had seen Godfrey in many moods—gentle with the sick, firm with the frightened, calm in the administration of justice and courageous in making up his mind; but here was another Godfrey, the leader who was bound to reach Jerusalem, the fighter who would drive an enemy into a corner and plunge a dagger into his heart. He wore the chain mail, all the linked rings that Bennet's father had fitted together so painstakingly back in the armory at Bouillon; but even the work of Papa's hands looked unfamiliar and strange to the boy.

In the days to follow Bennet would wonder often if the mild, gentle master would ever be seen again. Godfrey was ruthless now. Between Philippopolis and Adrianople the river ran through a pleasant grassy plain narrowed at times by mountains and populated with villages. It had been Godfrey's way to salute such villages with a dipping of the standards; but now swift riders left the ranks and charged through the carefully tended fields, leaving the huts aflame behind them. So complete was the desolation that Godfrey, who had ordered it, turned away sickened by the sight.

"What does God think of me for doing this?" he asked a priest once in Bennet's hearing. "I have committed sins higher than the heavens!"

"You must speak to Alexius in a language he can understand," the priest said. "Words did not impress him. Perhaps destruction will."

"Then may it be soon!"

At Adrianople a messenger from Alexius rode headlong into camp. Hugh had recovered from his weariness and would end his visit to the emperor as soon as the army was peacefully encamped at Constantinople.

"So now I can sleep tonight!" Godfrey said to Bennet. "Have Laurent sound the oliphants for a council. There will be no more pillaging of the country!"

The following morning the march was resumed in good formation, and on Christmas Eve of 1096 the Lorrainers reached Constantinople. Hugh's rakish followers, deprived of their leader, and the stragglers from Peter's mob had been encamped here for weeks, having themselves a carousing good time. But Godfrey looked up at the great double walls whch had kept the city of the emperor safe from attack for four hundred years, and shook his head.

"It will take more than superior forces to storm those defenses," he said. "We'll need all our nimble wits."

Very soon, Bennet would know what he meant.

CHAPTER SIX
THE GOLDEN CITY

Constantinople was a golden city. Everything about it seemed to glisten. Bennet, seated outside the blue silk tent which had been pitched on the lower slope of the mountain, looked down upon the garden-like place and breathed deeply of its strange scent. There was spice, possibly from the cargoes of the ships down in the Golden Horn, which hooked far up between the mountains to form a natural harbor off the Arm of St. George. There was the odor of the refuse accumulated in a great city, and stagnant water; but there was the perfume of the flowers which hid the refuse and the fresh air flowing down out of the green mountains. On either side of the Golden Horn the buildings clustered, white and squat, covered with vines and flowers. On the near bank, beyond the double wall, was the imperial palace. A great statue—of Constantine, Gareau had said—reared in majestic whiteness through blossoming trees. The gold dome of the ancient Church of of the Divine Wisdom shone in the sunlight and from its turrets the bells began to ring. Temple bells chimed at the same time, and camel bells jangled from a caravan winding around the mountain to the gate of St. Romanus. Back in Bouillon, Bennet thought, there had been only the chapel bell calling the villagers to Mass. All these different sounds were exciting.

And from inside the blue tent came excited voices. Hugh the Great was there, arrayed in the gold-embroidered tunic and cape which had been gifts from Alexius, the beautiful filigree bracelets clattering as he pounded the table before Godfrey. The emperor could buy Hugh's allegiance with costly presents, but he would find that Godfrey had no such vanity, Bennet thought complacently.

"Of course I don't trust him!" Hugh was saying now, and the bracelets whacked the table. "I know he would cut our throats on the instant if that would preserve his empire for him! But he knows the Turks are his greater enemy, and so he'll be our ally in order to fight them. In grinding our own ax, we grind his, too."

"If the only way I can get his help is to swear fealty to him, then I'll do without it!" Lord Godfrey declared.

"It's only words you're required to say!" Hugh implored. "I did it! I'm willing to employ any strategy to get to the Holy Land!"

"If I take an oath, I keep it," Godfrey retorted. "I have sworn fealty to the King of France, and I cannot accept another sovereign."

Bennet smiled proudly. But his attention wandered from the conversation, for down in the palace gardens just beyond the wall a peculiar wail arose, a wind instrument of some sort carrying a tune he never had heard before. The lament of it was tantalizing, as if a cobra might be swaying its hooded head to the rhythm.

Quietly Bennet gained his feet. He could not see over the wall. Lord Godfrey had given the order that no one was to enter the city. But a swift, secret run down the hill and straight back could hardly be called an entry. He glanced around. The other squires, awaiting their masters in the tent, were shooting darts at a broken cup set on a stump. Up the mountain and down to the river the haphazard settlement of tents and brush shelters was flung and there was activity everywhere, women washing clothes at the river, children playing, soldiers shooting dice almost under the feet of priests who strolled back and forth whispering their prayers. Below on the road the camels paced along to the open gate, their riders merely big lumps of drapery. Nobody ever would notice a boy shinnying up an ancient wall covered with vines. Bennet strolled down the slope. Then, nearing the wall, he darted into the cover of flowering shrubs.

Many vines had climbed the old stones and died in the six hundred years since the wall was built. Under the new growth there were dead stalks so thick that Bennet's groping toes found easy steps. Staying close to a giant plantain tree for cover, he wriggled up to the top, then swung across by means of vines to the second wall. The music was very near now, right below him. Lying flat on his stomach, he peered over into the garden.

It was like a story from the *Song of Roland*. Below the wall was a large shallow pool with the stones on the bottom painted blue so that the water itself appeared to be the color of the sky, and upon it floated pink and yellow water lilies as large as trenchers. Circling the lovely pool to where it lapped the wall was a marble walk and at the opposite side were wide, shallow steps. Along the steps were urns of growing flowers and ferns, with more steps going up into the distance from one overgrown terrace to another.

On the bottom step, with her bare feet touching the blue water, sat a girl. She had been making the music, for she had just taken the peculiar reed instrument from her lips. She was looking straight at Bennet across the short distance of the pool. Her hair was black as Hughette's, but not curling, and it hung in straight silk to her waist. Her dress was so thin that a pink fold of it floated as if a breeze blew, and it was caught only on the shoulders, leaving her arms bare. She wore a crown of roses and more roses were twined into the purple girdle around her waist. Purple, Bennet thought, purple for royalty? Could this be the emperor's daughter seated beside the pool with her bare feet in the water and her gold sandals lying beside her?

"Good evening," she said in French that had a sound to it like the temple bells. "Where did you come from?"

"Over the wall, milady," Bennet said before he thought. Now of course she would scream and a guard would come running.

But she only looked at him with curiosity.

"Then you're one of the Christians."

"I'm squire to Lord Godfrey."

"I've heard of him. He is a very bad man."

Bennet raised himself on his elbows. "He is a very good man!"

"Then why did he lay waste the country from Philippopolis to Adrianople?"

"Because the emperor didn't keep his word. He asked for help from the West and then imprisoned Hugh the Great."

"My father always keeps his word!"

"Your—father?" Bennet quavered.

"Alexius Comnenus, Emperor of the East. I am Anna Comnene. I can read and I can write well, and some day I shall write the whole treacherous story of what the Christians have done to my father!"

Bennet's stomach, pressed against the stones, was a sudden fearful emptiness. He had insulted the emperor's daughter!

She was regarding him haughtily. "My father asked help from the West because we will not be overrun by the Turks. But we will not be overrun by you, either! What lands you take back belong to us, not to you! The Holy Places are yours but Syria is ours!"

"Does the emperor think we came here to fight his battles for him?" Bennet demanded recklessly.

Anna tossed her pretty head. "Perhaps you will sing a different tune when your leaders speak to you from a dungeon!"

"Anna Comnene!" a cracked old voice called imperiously.

Bennet flattened himself on the wall. It would do no good because the girl would give him away and the old woman whom he could see plodding down the terraces would call the palace guard.

But there was only a torrent of Greek and the two voices receded. When finally Bennet dared look down from his skimpy shelter, the two figures were disappearing around a high-tossing fountain on the top terrace. He scrambled back across the bridge of vines to the outer wall and slid down the plantain tree.

In the silk tent Lord Godfrey was alone. He had stripped off the shoes with the laces that criss-crossed to his knees and he stood only in his smallclothes, washing himself in a silver basin.

"Where is my body squire, Bennet?" he asked as the boy entered, but before he could get an answer he added, "Lay out my blue tunic and cloak with the ermine collar. I'll appear before the emperor as a nobleman, not as a knight."

"Yes, Sire."

Bennet went down on his knees and opened the chest containing the fine clothes. But he did not take them out.

"Master, I have to ask you something!"

"What's on your mind, boy?"

"Are you going to take the oath of fealty to Alexius?"

"I'll take it for as long as I remain within his empire, he'll have to be satisfied with that. . . ." Godfrey, drying his big shoulders with the linen towel, turned as if only then did he realize the import of Bennet's question. "Why do you ask me such a thing?"

"Because—Sire, if you go to the palace you'll be walking into a trap! The emperor means to imprison you as he did Hugh the Great!"

Godfrey stared long at the boy on his knees before him. Then absently he folded his arms across the towel and sat down on the chest.

"Bennet, did you ever wonder why I chose you to be my stable squire?"

"Yes, Sire!" the boy replied so instantly that Godfrey smiled.

"I'll tell you why. Leroy is dependable and honest and loyal, so since he was of noble birth I had to make him my body squire. You are all of those things, and a little more. You have a—what shall we call it, recklessness—that Leroy doesn't know anything about. You'd take a great chance in an emergency, and you have judgment enough so that the odds would probably be in your favor. And that's why I chose you, boy. On the battlefield my life may at some time depend on your willingness to take a chance." He fingered the towel thoughtfully. "If I'm not mistaken, you took a chance today. That's how you found out the emperor's intentions."

"Yes, Sire."

"You have evidently saved me from imprisonment. However, I had given a strict order that none of my company was to enter the city."

"I didn't enter, my lord."

"Good!" Godfrey flung the towel across the tent. "Give me a linen shirt. Then run for my brothers. And ask Laurent to come in. I'll need a messenger. Our friend Alexius is due for a surprise!"

Bennet performed his duties so zealously that by the time he took his place outside the tent during the council his hair was on end, one stocking had slipped to his ankle, and his tunic looked as if he had gone swimming in it. But Lord Godfrey had praised him. More than that, he had expressed his trust and his expectations, and Bennet had never been so happy. Even when Leroy came stalking from among the tents with no explanation for his absence and stood looking down his nose at Bennet's rumpled attire, it made no difference. Inside the blue tent Lord Godfrey was giving Laurent the message for Alexius, and his full voice came plainly through the flimsy silk.

"Tell him we are not going to enter his city or visit his palace," Godfrey said bluntly. "Furthermore, we are not going to cross quickly into Asia as he has demanded. Our people are weary and they require rest. We'll remain here until the other armies arrive."

Laurent went off with the message. Alexius smiled as he listened, Laurent reported an hour or so later, and his reply was oily with polite friendship. But when the pilgrims tried to buy provisions the next day, all the markets were closed. "Very well, then we'll take what we must have to live!" Godfrey declared.

And the plundering began. Immediately the markets were opened. Once more the barley, fish, cheese, and bread were available but at three times the former price. Godfrey sent a complaint to the emperor, who replied that the prices would come down if the entire crusading army were to move into Pera, a large suburb on the north bank of the Golden Horn where many deserted buildings would give them shelter. Alexius did not have to point out that he would rest more easily with the harbor between himself and Godfrey. Since the rains and snows had begun and the people were cold in their makeshift shelters, the offer was accepted and a sort of armed peace descended on Constantinople.

The emperor, however, did not trust his guests. In every mountain pass a detachment of soldiers kept guard lest the Westerners stray out of Pera, and down on the river there was always a patrol of boats sailing slowly by. One bleak winter day a messenger slipped out of the dripping woods and up to the drafty castle occupied by Godfrey. He had come from the Dalmatian coast where the mighty Bohemund had landed with his forces. Bohemund asked that Godfrey withdraw back to Philippopolis and there await him, and in the spring they would make an attack together upon Constantinople.

"No," Godfrey said shortly. "Tell the Prince of Tarentum that we have not come so far merely to carry on the war his father had to abandon! We stay where we are and cross to Asia Minor with the first sign of spring."

The messenger slipped away again as quietly as he had come, unknown to the guards in the passes.

But there had been a second messenger sent also by Bohemund as insurance that his note to Godfrey would be carried through, and this one was intercepted by the guards. Alexius, remembering that Robert Guiscard had at one time threatened his empire and that Bohemund was his son, imprisoned the messenger and closed the markets. Once again the crusaders crouched beside fires that seemed to give no heat and listened to the hungry rumbling of their stomachs.

Angrily, Godfrey sent a protest to Alexius, reminding him that this army had done nothing to deserve such treatment and demanding that the markets be opened immediately. But the wet twilight turned to wet night and no sellers' boats appeared on the river and the market stalls remained empty. Alexius had threatened death to the disobedient.

Bennet had shivered through the chilly night on his pallet in the old hallway, sleeping fitfully and dreaming of his mother's porridge pot back home, and at dawn he stood up and stretched his cramped limbs.

"Where are you going?" Leroy asked from his place before Godfrey's door.

"Down to the river."

"There won't be any boats."

"We can see. There's no place else to get anything to eat."

The other squires, too uncomfortable to sleep, had gathered in the courtyard. Bennet and Leroy joined them, and in a running pack they covered the long slope to the Bathyssus River. Their breath hung in steam before their faces. The river's breath also hung in fog so dense that the bridge was only a few supports like the remains of a skeleton and there was no water at all. If some of the greediest sellers had anchored underneath the bridge, there was no sign of their boats. But in such fog a pirate brig could remain unseen. Upstream, hidden also, were the deep mountain passes where Alexius' archers listened and made no sound themselves.

The boys had been standing in a tight group, and now a few of them started forward.

"Wait!" Bennet said.

"What for?" Leroy asked. "There's nobody here."

Most of the squires stopped.

"It's quiet, isn't it?" said Lionel, who was old Lancelot's squire.

"Too quiet," Bennet agreed. "I don't even hear a bird. Let's go back."

"Who's scared?" Leroy jeered. "The sellers are waiting for us on the water!" And he ran on down to the bridge, followed by several boys.

Instantly, out of the fog shot a barbed rain. Leroy, in the lead, fell with an arrow in his shoulder. There was the thumping thunder of many feet on the bridge and a wildly yelling crew of men in long red Turkish trousers and steel helmets burst out of the fog, twanging their bows with deadly aim.

"The Turcopoles! Run!" Lionel shouted, and in the same second Leroy began to scream for help.

For one frozen instant Bennet stood still. The Turcopoles were the hybrid sons of Christian women and Turkish men, unruly by nature and perfectly fitted to be the emperor's warriors, so fiercely skillful with their short arrows that their very name paralyzed an enemy. A dark-faced one, teeth bared like an animal, rushed for Bennet. The boy ducked, caught him around the knees and threw him off balance, and the Turcopole rolled down the hill and landed with a splash in the river. Bennet tugged at Leroy.

"Get up! There's more coming! *Get up!*"

Somehow he dragged Leroy up the hill. Behind him,

doubly terrifying because nothing could be seen in the fog, he heard the screams of the squires who had been wounded and the wild yells of the Turcopoles.

Leroy was not badly hurt; but when Godfrey and his knights rushed down to the riverbank they found that several of the squires had been slain and the others carried off as prisoners. Bennet and Leroy were the only ones to escape.

"So this is Alexius' answer to my demands for food!" Godfrey said grimly. "All right, we'll not ask again!"

Through the old streets of Pera the oliphants called the general assembly, and Godfrey ordered the town to be vacated and then burned. Over the bridge where the blood of the young squires still had not been washed away by the rain, the army marched while the heavy smoke from the burning town blacked the sky behind them.

Once more Alexius could look over the wall from his palace windows and see the great swarm of the crusaders' tents and huts settled around his city. He retaliated by having his Turcopoles ambush and murder every party which left camp in search of food, and at the same time he sent Hugh the Great repeatedly to Godfrey to remind him that all would be peaceful if he would but take the oath of allegiance as Hugh had done.

"Never!" Godfrey thundered. "I will never become a slave like you!"

Hugh's great fists clenched and his breath came hard, but he made himself answer quietly. "I am not a slave. I only know that if we don't take Alexius' friendship as it is offered we'll never get to Palestine. He'll join with the Turks to defeat us."

"I'll never be his vassal!" Godfrey declared. "Bennet, tell Laurent to sound the call to battle!"

So the orders to form battle lines went out to all the weary and discouraged soldiers.

Alexius, that final day, presided over the battlefield in a manner to win the admiration of the knights. On a throne set up hastily within range of the fighting, he sat calm and unflinching even when the captain who shared the throne with him was felled by an arrow. All day the uproar continued, and when night came Godfrey ordered a rest.

Tempers were short after the long exertion and the squires argued among themselves as they waited in line for the cooks to fill their trenchers with supper stew.

"If Lord Godfrey would be sensible and take the oath, we'd have no more fighting," declared Arnold, who was Baldwin's squire.

"My lord is liege man to the King of France!" Bennet declared hotly. "He will never take an oath to a heathen emperor!"

"Lord Baldwin says it's stubbornness, not loyalty," Arnold retorted.

Bennet flung down the trencher and leaped at Arnold. The other squires instantly took sides and formed a shouting, dancing ring around the two who were now rolling in the dust. The cook whacked a head or two with a spoon but the boys paid no attention until Baldwin, hearing the fracas, ran over, jerked them apart, and took Arnold away with him.

"What were you fighting over?" Leroy asked with cutting sarcasm as Bennet, wiping his bloody nose, rejoined the line. "Lord Godfrey will take the oath tomorrow."

"He can't!" But a second later Bennet asked, "How do you know?"

"You'll see."

That was all Leroy would say. But he was right. The next day Lord Godfrey and all his companion leaders arrayed

themselves in their finest silk and ermine and rode their
bowing palfreys in through the Gate of Romanus. The squires
could go if they wished and see their masters take the oath
of allegiance to Alexius. Leroy, washed and combed, went
but Bennet hid himself behind the blue tent until the last
of the noblemen disappeared within the gate. Then he sat
down to brood, pulling up the trampled grass by the
handful.

He had quite a mound pulled when Gareau, trailed by
Cuthbert, wandered along and threw himself down in the
sun. His purple was nearly gray and his yellow was the hue
of a badly battered poplar and the white plume was a mere
stalk without a fringe, but he still had his jaunty air. Flat
on his back, he drew up one knee and rested his other foot on
top of it.

"Tactics," he said.

Bennet stopped pulling grass and looked at him, scowling.
Cuthbert nibbled at the heap.

"Our Lord Godfrey is employing strategy," Gareau went
on, squinting up at the sky. "He's a very wise young man.
He'll get much farther being Alexius' friend than his enemy."

"Alexius is not our friend!" Bennet blurted. "His own
daughter said so!"

"She did?" Gareau asked. But when the boy made no explanation, he continued, "Don't think Lord Godfrey doesn't
know all about craftiness. Just because he's honest and sin-
cere himself doesn't mean that he can't see through everybody else. In Greece, fight like the Greeks. Trade smile for
smile." He stopped again. "What's all the racket down by
the water? Is it worth sitting up to see?"

Bennet turned to glance down the hillside, then watched
with fixed attention. Along the road from Adrianople a new
army was advancing. A black gonfalon stood out smartly at

the head, black banners snapped from all the lances—and there appeared to be thousands of lances. Around the bend from the last mountain the knights rode rank after rank, fully armored, and after them came foot soldiers bearing swords and clubs, their shields brightly painted with lions and charging horses. At the head of the company, his yellow hair blowing in the wind, his palfrey as light-footed as if it had left home yesterday, their leader sat like a giant. He glanced at none of the people swarming down from the hillside.

"An enemy?" Bennet asked. "Will we be attacked?"

Gareau, who had sat up, laughed. "No! The mighty Bohemund, Prince of Tarentum, has arrived! And look who's with him! The gentle Tancred!"

"Where?" the boy demanded, but he hardly needed an answer. Beside Bohemund, armored and gloved, rode a young knight with a white scarf at his throat and a white banner tied to his lance. He still wore his blond hair in a crown of curls the way it had been when Bennet last saw him at Bouillon; but he was no longer a boy. He rode beside his uncle with the assurance of a fellow leader.

It appeared that the two would lead their army right into the streets of Constantinople and they were nearly at the gate when a great crowd surged suddenly out. Bohemund threw up his arm and the knights halted. In the midst of the crowd, mounted now on beautiful Arabian horses, could be seen Godfrey and his followers.

"Oho!" Gareau said softly, jumping up. "This we have to hear! Come, Bennet!"

All the people in the camp, it seemed, were running toward this interesting scene. Only Cuthbert, happily chewing at the mound of grass, remained on the hillside. Far enough up on the rise to see and hear well, Gareau and Bennet stopped. Behind Godfrey, disappearing into the crowd, was a long train of mules laden with packs, evidently gifts from Alexius. Bohemund stood in his saddle, looking over the mules. He was a powerful man of nearly forty, a head taller than the tallest of his knights, slender in the waist but wide shouldered and deep chested. In the bearded company he was conspicuous for being smooth shaven, conspicuous too for the savagery of his blue eyes and thin-lipped mouth. Meeting Godfrey's defiant regard, he laughed loudly.

"So you've taken the oath of fealty to the emperor!"

"I have not! I'll be his liege man only so long as I remain within the borders of his empire! I am loyal to the King of France!"

"Why didn't you wait for me, as I asked?"

"Why didn't you let me know you were coming?"

"I sent a messenger!"

"None came."

Bohemund's great fist smote his saddle. "So Alexius intercepted my messenger! He's up to his tricks again. What did you promise him?"

"To return his lands, if we take them from the Turks."

"Do you realize you've promised to conquer most of Asia Minor for him?"

Godfrey's handsome face flushed red. "I've promised only that in exchange for supplies we'll turn over to him whatever lands fall to us along the way! We did not come to win kingdoms for ourselves! Alexius will give safe passage to all the crusaders who come after us, and he will send us food and men whenever we need them. Isn't that worth something?"

Bennet's pride swelled so that it seemed to fill his throat. Lord Godfrey, in the blue silk cloak spread wide over his white horse, the edges thrown back to show the ermine lining, his brown hair shining, was a good match for Bohemund.

But Bohemund laughed. Spurring his horse so that it plunged and reared, he bore forward to the gate, scattering the people who had crowded in to listen.

"Where are you going?" Tancred asked.

"To visit the emperor! I'll beat him at his own game!"

"You can't fight him in the city!"

"Who wants to fight? I'm about to swear undying fealty to Alexius, Emperor of the East! Come, Tancred!"

"No! I'll have none of it!"

Bohemund, laughing uproariously, plunged past Godfrey, and his passage into the city could be followed by the screams of the people trying to get out of his way. A few of the knights followed. But when Tancred wheeled his horse to go back out along the road to Adrianople, most of them went with him.

"So the army from Tarentum is divided," Gareau said thoughtfully. "Bohemund keeps them alive and provided for by his nimble wits, but they follow Tancred." And he wandered up the hill after Cuthbert.

Bennet knew that Lord Godfrey was uneasy over Bohemund's arrival, for he slept very little that night. Before the break of day he aroused the boy, sending him through the camp to assemble the leaders. While Bohemund lingered at the palace vying in slyness with Alexius, the army commanded by the Duke of Lorraine passed over the Arm of St. George into Asia Minor, and with him went young Tancred and fifteen hundred of the knights who had followed him from the Dalmatian coast to Constantinople.

CHAPTER SEVEN
THE PIN OF THE PUSSYCAT

The crusaders did not remain long in the camp across the Bosphorus from Constantinople. Every day Bohemund, who was the go-between, brought a new and urgent message from Alexius.

"Move on," he said always. "The Westerners number too many now, and the food is giving out. March on to Nicaea!"

So when the forces of Count Raymond of Toulouse, with

Bishop Adhemar in the company, arrived under the old walls and were ferried immediately across the Arm of St. George, the leaders decided to take Alexius' advice.

Nicaea was the capital city of Bithynia in Asia Minor, the seat of the Turkish Empire of Roum, and it was ruled over by the Sultan David who called himself the Sword of the Lion. The sultan had overrun everything from the Orontes and Euphrates rivers to the shores of the Bosphorus, and now he had concentrated all his barbarous forces at Nicaea ready to storm Constantinople.

"In attacking Nicaea we keep the Turks busy so they can't march against Alexius, but we gain nothing for ourselves," said Robert of Flanders. "So why do it? Why not by-pass Nicaea and let Alexius attend to his own war?"

But when the army reached the fortress where a pitiful band of early crusaders had surrendered in good faith to the Turks and then been massacred, Robert of Flanders said no more. In the mountains they knelt while the priests said Masses over the bones of Walter the Penniless and his whole band. Peter the Hermit also had come this way and been swallowed into nothing. No force on earth, now, could hold back the avenging host. Over the vast plain full of moving people the sweet singing of the women and the praying of the priests and nuns hung above the thunder of hoofs and the everlasting creaking of the carts. Even the sick had no thought of turning back.

On the fourth day, so slowly that at first they looked like distant peaks spiking the far blue sky, the towers of the city of Nicaea began to rise. Excited shouts cut through the singing.

"Remember the Nicene Creed?" Gareau said to Bennet, his eyes on the far towers. "Seven hundred years ago the church fathers met behind those old walls and said, 'I believe

in God, the Father Almighty.' And now we're here because
we believe in Him too."

Bennet, standing in his saddle in order to see better, paid
little attention to the troubadour's educational remarks. He
wanted to see past the standards to the ancient city where
the Sword of the Lion waited. Falling back, he sent his palfrey
at a gallop toward a small brush-hidden creek on the far side
of which there was a low hill. From the summit he would be
able to see a little farther ahead.

The horse splashed into the water and lowered her head
to drink. Bennet, impatient, glanced down the stream.
Nothing to see there except a bundle of rags, the kind that
had been too common a sight back in Walter's camp. But
then, suddenly, the bundle began to move and whine. The
boy stiffened. Since the terrible incident back on the Bathyssus River, the squires had been warned to be cautious. But
as the bundle sat up and became a man, Bennet stared in
amazement, for the grizzled head turned, a shoulder went
up, and the whole face grimaced in a wink.

"Barb! Old Barb, it isn't you!"

The old fellow was trying to struggle to his feet and falling
weakly back. He wore only a rough sack belted at the waist
with a rope, but hugged tightly to his chest was the goatskin
cap with the little feet adangle.

Bennet jumped from his horse and ran across the slippery
stones.

"Barb, how did you get here? Where are the others?
Where's Peter?"

"I'm hungry, boy, starved. Knew you'd find me, knew it.
Put me on your horse."

And the old fellow held up a hand that was thinner than
Peter's which had waggled over the crowd by the river
Semois. Bennet jerked at him, trying to hurry, for Barb

was the first of the hermit's band to be discovered and he
would have a great deal to tell Lord Godfrey.

Holding Barb before him on the horse, Bennet rejoined
the ranks. Godfrey ordered the oliphants to sound an immediate halt. Someone produced a chunk of cheese, another a
piece of bread, someone else had a flask of wine. After Old
Barb had eaten, he recounted a story that had become too
familiar.

Peter the Hermit had been warned by Alexius that his
small band would be in grave danger but nevertheless he
proceeded on toward Nicaea, lingering to plunder along the
way. Knowing how the ragged forces were scattered, Sultan
David had sent a messenger to inform Peter that the city
had fallen to an advance expedition and was now in the
hands of his followers. The hermit had called together the
stragglers and rushed pell-mell over these very plains. David
permitted them to reach the walls of Nicaea. Then his warriors swarmed out of the gates and down from the mountains,
cutting and slashing. Except for a few with the craftiness
of Old Barb, every man, woman, and child had been murdered. Peter himself had not been seen since.

"And that Sword of the Lion, he's up in the mountains
right now, waiting for you," the old fellow warned, waving
toward the green humps beside the towers. "The Turks
don't fight like us, they don't draw up their armies and look
you over and then attack. No, sir, they pounce like cutthroats! And that's what he'll do to you!" And Old Barb
made a very realistic gesture of drawing his finger across
his throat.

Bennet's scalp prickled. In the May sunshine, with blackbirds twirring along the creek and colts neighing back
among the ranks of the mounted soldiers, it seemed im-

THE PIN OF THE PUSSYCAT

possible that bloodshed and death lay ahead on the blue horizon.

"Tell us about Nicaea, Barb," Godfrey said.

"Double walled, and each wall wide enough to drive a chariot on if you feel like it. And there's three hundred and seventy towers on top of it and great big ditches outside!"

"And Lake Askania?"

"It's around on the other side from here, gives them a chance to get out to sea. But it's full of weeds. You couldn't attack that way even if you had the boats."

"Then we'll march ahead, straight to the walls!"

"That's what Peter did!"

"Peter didn't have twenty thousand fighting men."

"The Lion has more, all up in the mountains! And he's left his wife and children in the city. He'll never let you take it!"

"We won't ask his permission," Godfrey said calmly. "We'll camp on the plains before the city until Count Raymond comes up with us. Then we'll attack." He raised his voice. "Sound the oliphants to advance!"

The horns blared and the army moved forward across the plains.

Even after the winter in Constantinople the purple banner of Lorraine and the blue gonfalon of Bouillon were bright. The noblemen still rode with falcons on their wrists, dogs trotted beside the mounted soldiers, the slow oxen with their carts brought up the rear. Children had been born on the way, some of the aged and the sick had died, and others had been left behind at the camp on the Bosphorus. The journey was not a picnic any more—the funeral grounds of Walter the Penniless had seen to that—but the crusaders had complete confidence in their own strength. Nicaea, the stronghold of David, would fall to them, then Antioch, the

Pearl of the East, and finally Jerusalem itself. The women sang again, marching toward the spear-pointed horizon.

Godfrey did not halt his standard bearers until it was possible to make out the masonry of the stout walls. To the north the mountains struck up to enormous, craggy heights. If David skulked there with his twenty thousand men, no sign of them could be seen. On the ramparts of the city the expected guards paced back and forth as casually as if the crusaders were another flock of blackbirds alighted for feeding. The only ominous sight was an unnatural hill where rags lifted and fluttered pathetically in the wind—the great heap of bones which were all that was left of Peter's band.

There were nineteen leaders, and they all came together around Godfrey's banner.

"Each of us should take a separate portion of the plain as camp ground," the duke suggested. "Then in the middle pitch a large tent where our priests can say Mass. Around it let's put up our other tents, like a town. The Sword of the Lion will see us as a city greater than his own!"

Baldwin wheeled his horse and made a face at the towering mountain. "That's what we think of you, Pin of the Pussycat! We'll come up there and pull your claws out in the morning!"

The men roared with laughter and shouted the new name until it was possible that David heard it in his mountain stronghold. Although he knew a squire should appear to hear and see nothing, Bennet could not help laughing. This would be a wonderful battle, this capture of Nicaea.

"We'll do no claw-pulling in the morning," Godfrey said. "We'll wait for Raymond. In numbers alone we'll outrank the Pussycat so badly that he'll have no heart for giving battle."

Baldwin grumbled. But he was outvoted. By night a new, far-flung city had blossomed on the plain.

The stars were still out when Bennet, asleep outside Lord Godfrey's tent, was awakened by a hand on his shoulder and Old Barb's beard brushing his cheek.

"Something's going on up there," the old fellow whispered.

Bennet, used to snapping from deep sleep into wakefulness, sat up instantly. "What's going on where?"

"The Pussycat's up to something. Want to come with me and find out what?"

Bennet never needed a second invitation to adventure.

The wind, cold as the breath of the Lion, swept down from the mountains as the two slipped past the sentries and out to where the horses were pastured. Horses might neigh but they had to have them for a quick retreat, Barb said. Riding bareback, they headed toward the enemy's hiding-place.

"I can't see or hear a thing," Bennet said. "Why do you think something's happening?"

"Smell it," Barb rejoined. "Here now, meanest place to get up, but they won't look for us to try it. Watch the ditch, there."

Barb seemed to find the way by instinct through the narrow slit where the mountain met the wall, then around impassable little canyons bottomless in the starlight, into passes so small that the rocky sides brushed the horses' legs, across wind-swept levels where nesting birds shot startled from the grass.

"Barb, we'll never find our way back!" Bennet protested at last. "We're lost——"

"Keep quiet. Leave the horses here. Go on foot now."

Bennet slid down to the unseen earth and tied the palfrey's

rein around a tree, stroked her nose in farewell, for he might never see her again, and then crept after Old Barb.

The trees were sparse now and the stars gave too much light for good cover. Bennet knew that they were on top of the mountain since there were no more heights above them. Suddenly Barb dropped flat and laid his ear to the ground.

"Thought so," he muttered. "Get into that thicket over there, quick!"

Bennet scrambled after him. They were no more than wormed into the thorny growth when he caught the faint beat of hoofs, a beat that grew into thunder as the first riders appeared. To the boy lying on a level with the horses' feet, the men were giants. Their helmets shone in the starlight. From under the helmets fluttered short white scarves and around their shoulders were short white capes. Catching the light at times were swords broad of blade and curved. The horses were slim legged and lean, bearing no weight of armor, nothing but the small saddle and the rider.

"The Pussycat's army!" Barb whispered against Bennet's ear. "Must be a million of them!"

"Can they see us?"

"Hope not! That's why there had to be two of us, one maybe will get away—lie flat!"

Bennet's flesh crawled as he pressed himself hard against the ground. Terrible stories of the Lion's treatment of spies had gone the rounds of the camp. He rubbed his tongue against his teeth. Cutting out your tongue was one thing they did. . . .

On and on came the riders, six abreast, so dark skinned they appeared to have no faces until the whites of their eyes gleamed. That eerie passage might have been a ghostly army except for the steady thump of the horses' feet.

The stars had paled into the dawn sky before the last rider passed. Barb lay still only until the scattered trees shadowed the white cape. Then, slipping and sliding and making no more noise than a squirrel, he led the way back to where the two palfreys waited.

"Do you know who those fellows are? Persians!" he said as they mounted.

"Where are they going?"

"Don't you know? Ride, now!"

The descent was swift, and as the horses came galloping out on the plain the sentries called to ask what had happened. Old Barb only waved and tore on to the blue tent where Godfrey, just awakened, wrapped himself in his cloak and came out to hear the news of the ghostly army.

"Persians!" he said. "So the Lion is scraping the far corners of his empire. Well, we'll not sit awaiting his pleasure. What of the lake, Barb? Have Alexius' boats arrived as he promised?"

"Nothing but weeds out there."

"Then we'll attack without him. Bennet, tell Laurent to order the call to arms!" But before he turned back into his tent, Godfrey laid his hand on Bennet's shoulder. "I won't forget this, boy," he said quietly.

That was all. But Bennet's feet had no weight as he ran to give his message to Laurent.

The oliphant sounded the hoarse call; then one after another the other horns caught it up and tossed it out over the plains like a stone skipping over water. Soldiers ran from their tents, the war chargers stamped, and the hauberks jingled as they were hastily thrown on.

Count Raymond's forces had come up during the night.

Tancred and Robert of Flanders and Robert who was the son of fighting William the Conqueror were more than ready for battle. With Godfrey in the center and the others flanking him, the crusaders made a courageous charge against the mountain.

Sultan David was not drawn out into the open. Shooting their wicked, short arrows with deadly aim, his warriors kept to the cover of the brush. Again an attack was made and again the ranks were driven back, carrying many wounded with them.

"Rest now," Bishop Adhemar advised at nightfall. "Let the Lion think you have given up. He'll come down of his own accord and you can fight him better on the plain."

The bishop was right. Through the night there was quiet, but in the early morning a screaming horde poured down through the mountain passes. The soldiers had slept in their mail. Hastily mounting, they met the attack with fury. Lances fell in ringing blows on helmets, arrows hissed through the air to snap against shields, cymbals clashed and horns tooted in the din that was part of the enemy's strategy.

Bennet had barely time to slip his hauberk over his head and snatch his blue scarf before Lord Godfrey was up and away. Through the battle he tried to keep somewhere near his master, but the duke was everywhere. The Turks, not so adept as the crusaders at hand-to-hand fighting, were driven back to the mountains.

"We have won!" the Lorrainers cried in triumph that night. "It is the will of God!"

But again at the break of day the Turks swarmed down from the mountains. The struggle lasted until darkness made it impossible to tell friend from enemy. Two thousand of the crusaders had fallen, four thousand of the Turks. Sultan

David dragged his weary forces back up to the heights and the army of the West settled grimly to prepare for the next day's battle.

Before dawn, however, Old Barb brought strange news to the blue tent. He had been up on the mountain in the very camp of the enemy. David was not resting. Into the passes leading to the north, away from the city, his army was spilling like a slow glacier.

"So he's giving up!" Godfrey exulted. "Now it's only a matter of time! We'll be over the walls in another day!"

But he reckoned without the desperation of the defenders holed up within the city. For seven weeks the siege went on. The crusaders built huge battering rams, then filled in the ditches and pushed the rams against the walls; but men were crushed beneath the timbers as the crude structures burned and fell, and others took their places only to be shot down by the marksmen on the ramparts.

"I'll undermine one of their own towers!" old Raymond declared. "It can't stand on air!"

With heavy losses in his ranks he carried out his threat, and in the night the tower tore away from the wall and fell with such mighty thunder that the earth shook. Into the gaping hole the soldiers rushed but were driven back by balls of fire, and by morning the break was repaired enough to hold back attack.

Around on the lake the boats promised by Alexius finally appeared. They had been carted overland and launched in darkness, and now they lay thick as ducks among the weeds. On every boat were fifty Turcopoles carrying banners and trumpets and drums. During the same night Bohemund had completed his march from Constantinople and encamped with his army on the plain. With him was Alexius' sergeant, Taticius, at the head of a small band of soldiers.

The crusaders, heartened by this new aid, agreed with Taticius that another attack should be made at once, and at the first daylight a charge was directed against the wall. Almost with the charge a banner appeared on the ramparts —the standard of the Emperor Alexius.

"The city has fallen!" Taticius cried, and led his men to the nearest gate which opened as if they had been expected.

The bewildered leaders drew together around Godfrey's standard.

"How is it that we besiege the city for seven weeks without success, but almost in the hour that the Greeks arrive, it falls?" Baldwin demanded.

"By all the stars in the heavens, there's been treachery somewhere!" Raymond roared. "Alexius has snatched our city from us! I'll slit his fat throat before I'll see him take the spoils!"

"What did you know of this?" Robert of Normandy demanded of Bohemund. "You came straight from Constantinople. Are you the emperor's man?"

Bohemund's hand reached for his sword, but Godfrey stopped him.

"Don't let your tongues be too swift! Let's hear what Taticius has to say for himself."

But Taticius was inside the city and the gates were closed to the crusaders. That night, Old Barb came with final word of the emperor's trickery.

"That Greek around on the lake, they call him Butumites, he's been making regular trips into Nicaea for a week! He told the Pussycat's guard inside that their only escape was in surrendering to him. To show them he meant it, he smuggled the royal family out to safety in the mountains, and then all the guards laid down their arms. And that Taticius, he led an attack just to make us believe that was how the city fell!"

The blue tent quivered with roars of anger from Baldwin and Eustace and the two Roberts. Old Raymond choked over his opinion of Alexius and even young Tancred who had wanted to be a monk gave way to rage. Bennet, crouched in the shadows beside the pallet upon which he would find no rest tonight, saw all the flushed faces in the candlelight and thought of another face. The emperor's daughter would be laughing, her haughty head tossing in enjoyment of the cruel joke her father had played on the hated Westerners.

"Make him pay us the full price of the spoils he will take in the city and let's be on our way!" Bohemund cried. "Alexius cares nothing for money! He wants Nicaea. I say give it to him!"

"I agree," said Godfrey, whose anger had kept him silent. "We did not come to conquer domains for ourselves. Fix a stout price and the money will get us to Jerusalem!"

The argument went on all night, but Godfrey won out. As the last of the council finally left the tent, he turned to his weary squires. Leroy had fallen asleep.

"Because of what you told me about the girl in the garden, I stuck to my belief that it's better to make the emperor pay with money than with more lives," the duke said to Bennet. "We know Alexius has a double tongue. He crossed us neatly this time. But not again!" Godfrey rose and walked slowly to the tent opening. The sun was coming up and the rosy sky framed his head—the uplifted head of a warrior. "Now, on to Jerusalem!"

"Amen," Bennet whispered to himself. The praise from his master was the accolade of the knighthood he would earn in the Holy City.

After a few days' rest the army again moved forward. It was a little smaller now, for there were graves left behind on the plains and a good many wounded to lie groaning in the carts. The march would be through enemy country and there were no guides to be had except for those sent by Alexius who, in spite of the incident at Nicaea, still protested his friendship.

"We'll do the scouting for Master Godfrey, you and me!" Old Barb said to Bennet with a wink and a shrug. "We're smarter than all the Greeks put together!"

"They won't trick us," Bennet agreed.

But they would soon know that up in the mountains through which they must pass, and out across the burning plain, the Lion was gathering his forces again. Fifty thousand strong, the Sultan was making ready to fall once more upon the trusting crusaders, and the Greek guides apparently knew nothing of it.

CHAPTER EIGHT
DEATH IN DORYLEUM

Leaving the plain before Nicaea, the army split into two
bodies. The largest, commanded by Godfrey, Raymond and
Bishop Adhemar, Hugh the Great, who had so long been a
reluctant guest of Alexius, and Robert of Flanders set out
across the Plain of Doryleum. To their left several miles
distant, following the course of a little river, marched Bohemund, Tancred, and Robert of Normandy. It was the end of
June and the sun was hot only in midday, and all the valleys

blossomed with flowers. The Greek guides made impressive trips off across the meadows on their swift ponies, returning to assure Godfrey that nothing but ducks and wrens disturbed the peace out there; but Old Barb listened with winks and shrugs, and when a campground was selected, green beside a river, he shook his head until the little feet rattled on the goatskin cap.

"Let's take a look around, boy," he said to Bennet. "Too quiet. I don't like it."

Bennet followed willingly enough, for the blue tent still remained on the cart and it would take time for the servants to unload and make camp.

They rode out to the low hills hemming in the valley, then up through underbrush, around sunny meadows and into deeper woods. No sound came to them aside from the rustle of their own passage and the songs of thrushes.

"There's nobody here," Bennet said finally. They had come out on a hilltop and the camp below was showing cooking fires. "Let's go back. I'm hungry."

Old Barb scowled at the green oaks. "I thought sure that Lion was around, playing Pussycat again. He wouldn't give up——"

The old fellow broke off. Under the oaks there was a sudden crashing and out into the clearing rode three Turkish soldiers. In their brown fists were the curved blades which in one blow could cut entirely through a man. Their scarlet tunics and white trousers were soiled from long wear, the horses had the leanness of much travel.

The three said nothing, but one rushed forward with his scimitar upraised. A quick word from the leader was all that saved Barb. There was a short and angry argument, then a swift movement of the horses, and Bennet and Barb were surrounded. At swords' points they were forced to ride in under the oaks.

They came in a short time into the enemy camp. The Turks did not bother with tents. On the hillsides as far as the eye could see, men lay snoring and horses grazed. There were no campfires. This was an army on the march. Below, a half-hour away, the crusaders laughed around the stew-pots while the shields and the mail lay with the swords on the grass.

Bennet never prayed more fervently than in the interval during which the three soldiers argued with their leader, and all the others who were awake came to join in the discussion.

"They can't agree on when to kill us," Barb muttered once, but the guard waved his scimitar so threateningly that he did not speak again.

Suddenly the debate ended and a half dozen of the fierce, dark-skinned men leaped into a circle around the two prison-ers. Bennet clenched his teeth and held his chin high. Lord Godfrey might know some day that his squire had died like a true knight.

But the flashing blades only cut the air, driving the captives before them into a small cave. A great stone was rolled over the opening, sealing them in. Then the voices receded.

Bennet's knees gave way and he sat down on the rocky floor.

"Barb, why didn't they kill us then?"

There was very little light but enough to show the gray-ness of Old Barb's face above the matted beard. He too had sat down and in his arms he hugged the goatskin cap.

"I couldn't get it all, boy; I don't follow their jargon well enough. But they've been snooping around, they know you're

Godfrey's squire, and I guess they think you're worth more alive than dead. Hostages are pretty fair barter in this kind of war." He looked around the cave, sniffing. "Jackals."

"Where?"

"This is a jackals' den. I can smell 'em. They'll be back as soon as we get out."

"Get out? Hah!"

"We will, don't you worry. Keep quiet now, let me think."

Barb took a long time to think. There was a crack of light around one side of the stone and it had grown dim before Barb at last stirred and looked out.

"He's there, boy. We'll have to be awful careful, digging."

"We can't dig around the rock. He'd see us."

"Here." Barb tapped the earthy ceiling. "Jackals don't burrow deep. Too lazy. We can make us a hole, easy. But no noise."

Kneeling beside Barb, Bennet went to work. His nails broke and his fingers bled, but when he felt grass roots he was rewarded.

"We've made it, Barb!"

"Oh, no, we haven't! Now's the time to be extra careful. We got to pull the grass down here in one big clod."

"Why, Barb?"

"Don't talk, work!"

The chunk came down, and the round patch of stars framed in the opening was the most beautiful thing Bennet ever had seen.

"Now make the hole a little bigger, so I can rise up," Barb said. "I'm going to fling this clod out so's it'll roll down the hill. In the dark the fellow'll think it's us. And while he's chasing it, we'll make our escape. Ready?"

Barb, with the clod held against his chest, wriggled up until his shoulders were free. In the black dark Bennet could not see, but suddenly, outside, the Turk gave a shout and they could plainly hear him charging off down the hill. With the boy pushing from below, Barb wriggled out of the hole, then pulled Bennet after him. They dared not try to find their horses. On foot, with only Barb's instinct to guide them, they crept through the woods and down the mountain.

They had been obliged to stop and reconnoiter so many times that it was daybreak when they reached the camp. Lord Godfrey had not lain down in the blue tent. He had hardly heard the account of the capture before he ordered the oliphants to sound the rising signal.

"They'll attack us, or if not us, then Bohemund over in the other valley. We must join forces immediately!"

Yet it had to be a slow advance, as slow as the oxen drawing the carts, for they dared leave no one behind as a target for the Turks. Past midday Barb, scouting ahead, came galloping back to confirm their fears. The Lion had fallen upon his prey. An hour's ride farther on, in the little valley of Doryleum, Bohemund was fighting desperately beside a small river swollen red with blood. The knights, well protected by their shields and armor, had withstood the first attack with few casualties but their horses had fallen like sparrows. Unmounted, the knights were now at the mercy of the Turks who, on their swift horses, darted in with slashing swords and away again before they could be touched. Robert of Paris had fallen, Tancred had been in terrible danger when his lance broke and he was left without a weapon until Bohemund rushed in and rescued him. Tancred's brother William was mortally wounded. Many of the women had been carried off by the attackers.

"We'll delay no longer!" Godfrey declared when he heard this news. "Laurent, order the assembly of the cavalry! We'll leave the foot soldiers to protect the carts. For every mounted knight and soldier, on to Doryleum!"

Bennet snatched Lord Godfrey's lance and sword from the cart. Within minutes the blue standard of Bouillon and the purple of Lorraine moved ahead, whipping in the breeze of furious haste.

From the top of the hill beside Lord Godfrey, Bennet looked down upon a scene he would never forget. Bohemund's camp had been formed into a circle but it had proved no defense against the wildly charging Turks. Many of the carts had been set afire and the smoke of burning grain lay hot in the air. The grassy hillside was slippery with the gore of battle. A clump of yellow flowers waved foolishly over a heap of broken lances. The knights' colors were only small dots among the waves of scarlet and white of the Lion's warriors.

Waiting only long enough for his knights to assemble, Lord Godfrey led the charge down the hill. Bennet, remaining behind on the hilltop with the other squires, saw the blue gonfalon above the helmeted heads, steady and high in the hands of Laurent. The Turks, wheeling to face the armed and shielded ranks pouring over into the valley, made a frantic attempt to break through. After a day of continuous fighting they were no match for these fresh forces, and now they were only trying to save their own lives. Curved scimitars rang against breastplates, men shouted and horses screamed, sometimes the shriek of a woman slipped high above the din. The Turks, undoubtedly weary, were nevertheless taking a toll among the crusaders.

"Look!" Leroy exclaimed suddenly beside Bennet. "It's going down!"

Bennet, not having to ask what he meant, looked toward

the blue gonfalon. It was wavering as if Laurent had been wounded and could not support the weight of its staff.

"Laurent, hold on!" Leroy shouted, and without hesitation sent his horse plummeting down the hillside into the very heart of the battle.

Gareau, on Cuthbert, had come up in time to see the brave deed.

"Never let the gonfalon touch the ground!" he said. "He's caught it!"

The blue fluttered high again. It was impossible to see what happened next, for men and horses were jammed in a struggle around the banner; but suddenly the standard was gone again. The yells of the Turks increased because they knew from other battles that the loss of a gonfalon might mean the crumbling of an army.

"Lord Godfrey! *Where is he?*" Bennet cried. "Gareau, can you see him?"

Trying to single out one helmeted head from another was like trying to distinguish one grain of sand on the seashore. A leader always remained near his gonfalon so his men would know where to find him. The Duke's silver helmet and blue-bannered lance had been there a minute ago. Had Godfrey gone down also in that twisting fray?

Slashing his horse with the reins, unarmed and bare-headed as every squire must be, Bennet rushed headlong down the hill. Through struggling men and crazed horses he fought his way to the spot where he had last seen the gonfalon. Lord Godfrey, without his helmet or lance and with his shield dented by many blows, was on the ground astraddle a huge Turk.

"Bennet, a weapon!" he cried.

Bennet jumped from his horse, jerked a scimitar from the hand of a dead enemy, and threw it to him. He didn't wait to see what Godfrey did with the sword. A short distance ahead Laurent lay with his eyes open to the sky. Beyond him was Leroy, doubled over to protect something with his body. Bennet knelt and rolled him over. Underneath him was the crumpled banner of Bouillon, its blue stained with bright patches of red.

Hastily Bennet lifted the staff to his shoulder and felt the tug of the wind.

"It is the will of God!" he shouted.

The knights near him caught up the cry and it echoed through the little valley.

From that moment the battle turned. Completely routed, the Turks scrambled on foot or on horseback up the hillsides. The knights, not content with driving them out of the valley, pursued at a full gallop. Within minutes the valley was empty except for the women who knelt weeping over the groaning wounded and the priests praying beside the ones who did not groan.

Bennet's horse had run away. With the banner held high, the boy climbed slowly to the hilltop. Plunging the staff into the ground, he sat down where the blue folds could brush his shoulder.

He was still there at dusk when the knights returned from their long chase after the Lion, and Lord Godfrey thundered up on his great war horse. Dismounting, the duke dropped the rein over Bennet's arm and pulled off his helmet.

"Sire, you said once that I had more courage than Leroy," the boy began at once because he must say all the things he had been thinking. "I haven't. He went to help Laurent. I didn't. He died with the courage of a knight!"

"Who carried the gonfalon here to the top of the hill?" Godfrey asked quietly.

Bennet drew the reins through his fingers. Godfrey turned

to face the wind, letting it lift his moist hair, and now he was looking directly down into the terrible little valley.

"Boy, don't grieve for Leroy. His part of the crusade is accomplished. Ours is not. But because of him, and hundreds like him, tomorrow we march on toward Jerusalem!" He laid a hand briefly on Bennet's shoulder. "Take the horse to Louis. Then come to my tent. You'll have to take Leroy's place, be my body squire. He was a good one!"

And Godfrey walked away leaving Bennet rather stunned behind him. The body squire was the highest in rank because he rendered such personal service to his master. Bennet had longed for that coveted post. But, remembering Leroy's sacrifice, he was hardly happy about it now.

The next morning four thousand of the crusaders were buried in unmarked graves. Bennet watched carefully during the service and he knew where they laid Leroy. There was one last thing he wanted to do. The gonfalon had been slashed by a sword in the battle and from the tattered end of it he had torn a small ribbon. When the people turned away from the newly made mounds, he knelt and with a bright red twig pinned the little blue strip to the earth that covered Leroy.

Riding off, he looked back. The tiny blue fluttered as bravely as when it was a part of the proud gonfalon of Bouillon.

CHAPTER NINE
THE FOUR HILLS OF ANTIOCH

Unwilling to face the crusaders again in open battle, the
Lion skirmished ahead of them across the plain where the
August heat made shimmering lakes in the distance. What
food the country might have furnished was laid waste, every
village burned and every field flattened. The wells were
poisoned and the rivers had dried up in the heat. Yet the
courage of the army never wavered. Roots of wild plants
and a few small fields of corn were all the food they had.

THE FOUR HILLS OF ANTIOCH

There was nothing for the horses. The line of march was marked painfully by the carcasses of horses, dogs, pigs, and donkeys, and by more graves heaped with rocks against the jackals. Falcons disappeared, either liberated to hunt their own food or killed and eaten. Belted knights, who would have considered it dishonor to walk in France, trudged along in linen tunics while their squires carried the chain armor and leather shirts which were unbearable in the heat. Some rode oxen and camels. Old Barb, mounted on a camel, scouted out and around the army. Noticing one day that a few dogs returned from a foraging expedition with muddy paws, he followed their tracks and found a small river. The water saved some lives while others were lost in the mad scramble.

Not until the two favorite leaders were stricken did the people complain. Count Raymond became so ill that he was given Extreme Unction and his young wife besought heaven to spare him to her and her infant son. Godfrey encountered a bear in a thicket and was clawed badly before Bennet, snatching the knife from his master's belt, drove the animal away. The crusaders prayed for them frantically, and the complaints became as loud as the prayers. They would have met defeat at the hands of the Lion rather than lose Raymond or Godfrey. Even the sight of fertile forests and wide-flowing rivers, and eventually the city of Antiochetta, did not lift their spirits. The city welcomed the Westerners as conquering saints, giving them food and wine. But there was no rejoicing until the day Lord Godfrey at last opened his eyes and asked for food, and those who cared for Raymond sent out word that the count had made a truce with death and would not die until Jerusalem had been liberated. Then the joy was boundless, and Bennet, who had watched without food or rest beside his master, fell asleep in the blue tent with Gareau's happy song ringing in his ears.

After a few days' rest, the march was resumed. Bohemund and Tancred were sent out ahead toward Iconium with Baldwin following, for the leaders were determined that a short food supply would not plague the crusaders again and the best insurance was to break the army into smaller bodies. Bohemund reached Tarsus, the famous birthplace of St. Paul, and his gonfalon flew on the walls until Baldwin, coming up with superior forces, declared that the city should be his. The dispute mounted into bloodshed and in the end Bohemund and his young nephew departed, to rejoin the general army much later at Marash. Baldwin, delighted with the easy conquest he had made, continued on from Tarsus to the Christian stronghold of Edessa, where he made himself king and never again took up the cause of crusade.

Before reaching Marash, the main army must cross the great mountains of the Taurus. On the plain called "burning Phrygia" by the ancients, the crusaders had died from heat and thirst. Now, ascending into the mountains, they came into desolate, snowy wastes. Once again the knights put on their leather shirts and mail for warmth, the women wrapped themselves and the children in everything that had been carried in the carts, but nothing could protect them from the bitter winds. In Lorraine there had been snow, melting at the first touch of the sun. Here there was no sun. Snow as piercing as needles whipped down from the rocky summits, driving the horses into a mad plunging that toppled them off the narrow rock ledges and over the precipices. The camels, whose soft feet were made to spread on desert sands, whined and balked and moved on over the cold rocks only at the lash of the whip. The foot soldiers cast their weapons into the canyons and declared they would go no farther.

"But what is there for you here?" Godfrey asked them. "Is there food? Shelter? Taurus is the worst of the mountains. After this we cross Amanus and then we're into Syria. Don't give up now!"

The men, groaning, dragged themselves on. Each night, when the cold darkness stopped them, Bishop Adhemar would walk among the miserable people, blessing them and urging them to pray. Morning, noon, and night camel bells captured from the Turks were rung and along the struggling lines the Angelus was said. The crusaders would never again be as close to one another in brotherhood as in these terrible days. By common consent there was no stealing, beggars gave instead of asking, knights walked while sick servants rode.

"Our heights of misery have lifted us nearly to paradise," Gareau observed. "I wonder, will we continue on as different men when we come down into the sun and wealth of Syria?"

Gareau was answered at Marash. Tancred and Bohemund were at the meeting place with the news that Baldwin had made himself King of Edessa. Some of the leaders grumbled jealously over his good luck, others said the army was well rid of him. Godfrey was furious, but none knew better than he that Baldwin had come on crusade to gain a kingdom for himself. Now let him go.

Revived by the warm weather and plentiful food, the army moved on to the south. Their spirits were high until, nine miles away from Antioch, they came upon a seemingly impregnable bridge over the Orontes River. The span was of nine stone arches, each with its iron-plated gate. Rank upon rank, the army halted while the leaders came together to discuss what should be done about this unexpected barrier.

"I knew there would be a stoutly defended bridge over

the Orontes," said Robert of Flanders, "but this is the equal of nine separate bridges because each span must be stormed and taken by itself!"

"So now we'll be forced to rot here for weeks, working our way inch by inch, while the Turks prepare well for siege at Antioch!" fumed Robert of Normandy. "Look at them over there, the dogs!"

He glowered at the far bank where a large band of Turks was drawn up, well out of arrow range. Behind each of the gates there would be more of them, perfectly protected by the iron plates.

Godfrey appeared not to be listening. He was gazing up the near shore toward some low hills. Bennet turned to see what had drawn the lord's attention. It was a company of beggars, if one judged from their rags blowing in the wind. Hurrying apparently from a hideout in the hills, falling and stumbling and even crawling, they swarmed across the grass toward the group around the blue gonfalon.

The man in the lead was familiar to Bennet. His beard was longer and his hair more matted than when he had been on the bank of the Semois, and his rough wool garment was worn to ribbons; but his lean brown face was the same and he shouted with the same enthusiasm as when he had first urged the crusade. It was Peter the Hermit.

"Thank God you have come! We have been waiting for you, we never gave up hope! Welcome, welcome, my lords and people, welcome to the hardships and glories of God's work in the Holy Land!"

"But they killed you!" someone cried in the astonished silence. "You all died back at Nicaea!"

"God preserved us in a truly wonderful fashion," Peter replied. "The enemy took us for dead but when they departed from the field we dragged ourselves into the hills.

Eventually we discovered one another and made our way this far by the help of kind Christians who live back in the mountains. And now God has us to help you to Antioch! Praised be His Holy Name!"

Questions were rained upon Peter, but he held up his scrawny hand. "In God's good time, I'll tell you all that has befallen us. But not now! We must take the bridge!"

"How?" asked Robert of Normandy, and the other leaders echoed it.

"How? By storm! You can take it in a single charge!"

Bennet saw Godfrey shake his head, but Robert was already calling to his squire to bring up the war horse and his body squire was running forward with his shield and lance.

"My men and I will do it alone!" Robert cried. "Stand back, you fainthearted ones, and watch! It is the will of God!"

Robert was as good as his boast. In a brilliant sally he drove the enemy from the bridge, the Christian army passed over, and the arches were blocked behind them with stones. Then, with trumpets sounding and banners flying, they advanced to within a mile of Antioch and camped. The Turks, remembering the fall of Nicaea, fled into the city and barricaded the gates.

That night, in Godfrey's blue tent, a council was held among the leaders. The night was mild and the tent flap was open, and Bennet squatted outside where he could watch and listen. The other squires were shouting over a wrestling contest for which Gareau was referee, and sometimes it was hard to hear what went on in the tent. But Peter the Hermit held the floor. In the light of the candle he pounded the table and shook his bony fist as he had on the bank of the Semois.

"Don't wait! Attack at once!" he urged in his high treble. "You've surprised the enemy by advancing so quickly. Now make use of the surprise!"

There was an awkward pause. The princes, lolling on the rugs taken from the Lion's last camp, had overeaten and they were drowsy except for Godfrey and the emperor's man, Taticius. Godfrey was alert and attentive, but it was Taticius who followed every word of Peter as if he must memorize it to report back to Alexius.

"Antioch is truly the Queen of the East," Peter went on. "Two leagues or so to the east is a marvelous lake whose waters run down through the city and join the Orontes on this side. The enemy will never lack for water. Or food. The Mountain of Orontes is covered with gardens and country houses well stocked with fruit and grain. You can't starve them out!"

"What of their defenses?" Eustace asked lazily. He was stretched full length on Godfrey's bed, his hands clasped behind his head, half asleep.

"The city is built on four hills, and on the western hill there is a citadel, strongly walled, and from its walls the archers can fend off attackers from every direction. The ramparts which surround the city itself, including the citadel, are impregnable. The towers alone number three hundred and sixty! And in addition there is the great Black Mountain on the north, a natural, rugged defense; and between us and the wall on this side is the river Orontes and wide soft marshes and the great ditches dug for protection!"

"In spite of all these defenses, Antioch has been taken," Stephen of Blois said thoughtfully. "The Saracens had it once, then the Greeks. And only fourteen years ago the Turks conquered it and are still in possession. Are we weaker than they?"

Bohemund, huge in his gold-embroidered red, jumped up to pace the small area around the table.

"We can take Antioch! Tomorrow!"

"Tomorrow, yes, and by the day after tomorrow you'd be governor of the Pearl of the East!" old Raymond sneered.

"It will not be taken tomorrow," Bishop Adhemar broke in, always ready to avert a quarrel. "Accien, who is the grandson of the sultan who conquered Antioch fourteen years ago, is holed up there with seven thousand horsemen and twenty thousand foot soldiers. If by chance the outer walls should fall, he would take refuge in the citadel, and it would be impossible to rout him from there except by famine. And Accien is well prepared for us, you may be sure. We'd starve before him."

"Then what do we do?" Godfrey asked. It was the first time he had spoken.

"Wait until spring," said the bishop, but immediately there was a storm of protest. He raised his battle-scarred hand. "Yes! In the cities around Antioch we can find a friendly reception, for as Peter has told us, there are many Christians in this part of Syria. Then in the spring we'll be ready."

"I'm not afraid of the Turks!" Bohemund said rudely.

"Neither am I," the bishop said so gently that the big man flushed. "But I do fear the rains and the winter winds and the terrible sight of our people dying from starvation."

"But if the city were to fall soon," Godfrey put in, "then we would have the fat of the land through the winter. And we'd be catching Accien before he could organize his forces for a proper defense."

"By spring we'd be strengthened by new arrivals of crusaders," added Robert of Flanders. "And Alexius has prom-

ised us boats full of provisions to land at the Port of St.
Simeon—how far away? Three leagues?"

"Alexius!" Bohemund snorted. "We'll be fortunate if he
doesn't join forces with Accien!"

Angry voices tumbled over one another inside the tent
and it seemed to Bennet that there would be a rough and
ready fight. He turned to look off toward the four hills of
Antioch rising beyond the walls and was startled to see a girl
standing very near. Her eyes were darker than ever in her
pinched face. She had the look of a Madonna with a baby
in her arms and a small boy clinging to her ragged skirt.
Her feet were wrapped in tatters of leather, the children
were barefooted. The only beauty remaining to her was her
hair, long and black and curling.

"Hughette?" Bennet asked as if he could not believe his
senses. "Hughette, are you ill?"

She looked at him a long time. "I've been ill since the
Taurus. My mother died back there. My father was killed
at the bridge today." She made a gesture toward the children. "I don't know what to do with them."

"Who are you, child?" Godfrey asked, for he had come
out of the tent to get away from the quarreling. The kindness in his voice started the tears running down her face.

"She is Hughette, daughter of the tanner, Sire," Bennet
replied. "She says Victor was killed at the bridge."

"And she's alone?"

"Yes, Sire."

Godfrey whirled to the company in the tent. "Look at
this girl, will you, and then tell me we shouldn't attack
until spring! Are all these lives to have gone for nothing?"

The leaders crowded out of the opening. The two small
children also had begun to weep. Bishop Adhemar knelt,
drawing the little boy to him and stroking his hair.

THE FOUR HILLS OF ANTIOCH

"I was wrong in thinking we should delay," he said. "Antioch will fall to us. More than a thousand years ago the name of Christian was given to the world here, Peter was named the Rock and became the cornerstone of the new Church. Martyrs have died here, miracles have taken place. And now it is the will of God that we take Antioch back from the infidel!"

"We'll draw up the lines in the morning," Godfrey said, and there was a general murmur of agreement. He laid his hand on the girl's bowed head. "Take them to the wife of our standard-bearer, Bennet. Her own son died at Nicaea. She'll take care of them."

Then, with a gesture which left the others no choice but to follow him, he went back into the tent.

The next morning the army moved up into position for siege. Godfrey and Raymond crossed the river to the only solid ground between the marsh and the wall, and the other leaders took up their stand around the north sector to the mountains on the east. The great body of the crusaders, however, had no taste for fighting. In the hazy autumn sunshine they roamed through the laurel groves, found herds of sheep and cattle in the meadows to the north, wine and nuts stored in the deserted residences outside the walls, corn ready for plucking, and fig trees heavy with fruit in the forgotten fields.

"We've earned all this, now let's enjoy it!" the men grumbled.

Godfrey, Tancred, old Raymond, and Bishop Adhemar disputed them; but the voices of four men were nothing in a chorus of ten thousand.

While the crusaders sickened themselves with feasting, the Greeks under Taticius asked one another how long they had to put up with such folly. Accien, they knew, was well informed by his spies of all that was going on and was receiving supplies through the unguarded gates. The siege of Antioch, Taticius told the Emperor Alexius by messenger, was a joke and a disgrace. Because the thirty-foot-high walls remained empty of soldiers and the city itself was a vast pool of silence, all of the leaders except the four took it to mean that Accien was giving up in despair. In reality he was waiting for the winter rains to flood the plain between the river and the city wall, when it would be a simple matter to disperse the besiegers. Alexius had no taste for such a defeat, and so in early November Taticius and his garrison withdrew.

Almost at once the rains began, and the camps on the river bottom were flooded. At the same time the food supplies became exhausted and the Flemish pirates, upon whom the army now depended to send supplies up from Port St. Simeon, were themselves made prisoners by the Greeks. And these were the days when Accien chose to send swift horsemen darting out to attack and be gone again before any defense could be organized.

"We're a bunch of drowned and starving rats, and the dogs are after us," Gareau said.

Bennet, crouched beside a small fire that the rain kept putting out, laid on another wet stick and watched Hughette turn the small bit of meat in the smoke. If it were not for the foraging done by Old Barb and the scraps of plant roots Hughette dug, Lord Godfrey would have gone hungrier than the rest because he gave away everything of any account.

In these terrible days there were many deserters. Robert of Normandy left a gap at the Gate of the Dog when he slipped away to Laodicea. Other lesser leaders joined Baldwin who was now governor of Mesopotamia.

Desertions went on until Lord Godfrey ruled that death would be the price of flight, and there were no more escapes. Turkish spies were found in the camps and executed, but more spies remained undiscovered and word of pestilence and starvation, vice and wickedness seeped through to Accien.

"Let's give him news of another kind!" Bishop Adhemar suggested one day. "We'll plant our precious grain instead of eating it. When the Turk sees the growing fields, he will know we intend to stay for the harvest!"

But Accien looked out at the rows of green and instead of surrendering, sent hasty demands for help to all the neighboring sultans.

The crusaders met up with the relief forces in a manner they did not expect. A fleet of ships from Genoa and Pisa had anchored with supplies at Port St. Simeon, twenty miles away, and a great number of men mostly unarmed set out joyfully to buy provisions and to hear news from home. On their way back they were attacked and many were massacred by a troop of four hundred Turks. A few messengers, breaking away from the rout, flew to the camps. Immediately Godfrey ordered every available man to take up arms, and the army poured out over the bridge of boats they had maintained over the Orontes and on to the road to St. Simeon.

The fighting that day made up for all the laxity of the winter. Godfrey ordered the other leaders to follow him and he charged into the Turkish ranks. The enemy were not used to hand-to-hand combat and they broke and ran.

"Over there, Master!" Bennet cried from the hilltop where he had watched the battle, and pointed to the ravine where the Turkish horsemen had packed themselves into hiding.

With a wave of his lance, Godfrey followed. Never had

he fought as he did then. Cutting off their retreat to the city, he kept up the charge until not one of the enemy remained alive in the ravine.

Excitement was high that night, the sodden defeat of winter turned to unexpected victory. The fall of Antioch was at hand. Out on the plains the new green of wheat and corn was trampled by the triumphant merrymakers because now the harvest would not be needed. The army would be in Jerusalem by the time the summer sun ripened the crop.

But in the next few days, while the crusaders neglected to guard the gates, the besieged made sorties out through the Bridge Gate and the Gate of St. George, procuring supplies enough to keep the city from starving.

"Outwit us, will you?" old Raymond grumbled.

On the bank of the Orontes opposite the Bridge Gate, he built a tower and watched his men roll great building stones from a ruined mosque to seal up the gate. On a hill commanding the Gate of St. George, Tancred also threw up a tower of stones and timbers, and now the city was sealed into itself. From the brooding old citadel Accien glared down at his weakening people and tried to think up new means to goad them into holding out. For seven months the Army of the West had caroused and prayed and done battle outside his walls. The Queen of the East was in grave danger of becoming a specter of death.

"It's the time to attack, storm them down!" Old Barb urged, back from one of his secret excursions around into the mountains. "Why, the guards in the towers haven't the strength of babies! Antioch could be ours in a day!"

But even Godfrey shook his head. Bennet was a little ashamed of him. A few weeks ago the duke had been violently disgusted with his people for hanging back. Now it seemed he had become like all the others, indulging in petty quarrels.

"I don't know what has come over us," Gareau said sadly to Bennet as they stood watching the workmen erect a beautiful new tent on Godfrey's campground. "A month ago the duke wouldn't have fought over a tent."

"It was Bohemund's doing," Bennet reminded him with heat. "Baldwin sent the tent to Lord Godfrey from Edessa, and Bohemund stole it on the road! Of course my master wanted what was intended for him! Baldwin is his brother, King of Edessa, and if he wants to send Godfrey a present . . ."

"Did Godfrey act this way when we started out?" Gareau countered. "'It is the will of God!' Remember? But now God seems to be looking the other way."

Bennet, impatient at hearing even this well-deserved criticism of his master, turned and stamped away along the road which led past all the camps and finally around to the St. Paul Gate guarded by Bohemund. He would know later that when he turned in that direction, God was again looking toward the crusaders.

CHAPTER TEN
TRAITOR IN THE NIGHT

As he passed the camp of Robert of Flanders, which was next to Bohemund, a group of squires called to Bennet.

"We're going fishing in the river! Come with us?"

But he pretended not to hear. Leaving the road, he wandered up the slope toward Bohemund's tower and into a laurel thicket where he threw himself on the ground. All the blossoming trees perfumed the hillside, birds sang the last songs of the day, insects hummed in June drowsiness;

but none of it pleased Bennet. He was thinking rebelliously of the change in Lord Godfrey when a man spoke close beside him. Bennet jumped. But then he realized that not only had the man not spoken to him, but he was out of sight. The voice was unfamiliar. The voice which answered, however, was the deep, unmistakable baritone of Bohemund. Bennet had no intention of eavesdropping, but after he caught the first remarks he remained utterly still.

The strange voice spoke French with an eastern accent. The man's name was Phirous, and he was in command of the tower named the Three Sisters, adjacent to the blockaded Bridge Gate.

"I'm still a Christian at heart," the man whined, "I have never given up my God. But here I must live with the Turks and so I appear to be a Moslem!"

"Quite the right attitude," Bohemund agreed. "And you are a trusted soldier of Accien. Why did you send a message that I meet you here?"

"Sire, I'm a poor man——"

"Let's not waste time. What is your proposition?"

"The rule among your leaders is that the one who first plants his gonfalon on a city wall is to be the governor of that city, am I right, Sire?"

"That's an old custom in war. We abide by it."

"So if you and your forces could be first into Antioch, you would become its new governor. The Pearl is a great prize, Sire!"

There was a short pause, and Bennet lay without breathing. It was no secret that Bohemund coveted Antioch. But would he resort to trickery to get it?

"What is your price?" Bohemund asked after a moment.

"A hundred bezants now. A little more later."

"Why did you single me out from the other princes?"

"Because I have seen you often from the wall, Sire, and you stand head and shoulders above all the rest."

"And you know I want power!" Bohemund added shortly. "What is your own reason for selling out your Accien?"

"There is an army marching out of Persia and coming to his relief. If he is able to hold the city, I remain in his army, poorly paid as I am now. But if you take it, I'll be rich." The voice took on the whine again. "And I can once more be a Christian!"

"How do I get into the city?"

"I'll let down a ladder for you from the Tower of the Three Sisters, and you ascend. There is a small stairway down inside to another gate, unknown to your friends, beside the great Bridge Gate. If you were to open that little gate from the inside, surely you could say with truth that you were first into Antioch!"

"Are you sure you can manage this, Phirous?"

"On my honor, Sire!"

"I'd like a better oath than that," Bohemund said, but he sounded pleased. "Tell me your plan in detail."

"I'm not quite ready, Sire. Tomorrow at this time I'll meet you here, and by then I can give you directions. And you'll have the hundred bezants?"

"I'll have it!"

There were polite assurances from both plotters of their high esteem for one another, and then the brush rustled as they moved off in different directions.

Bennet lay still for what seemed to him a long time. Then, cutting back toward the river so that he came out of the woods far from the place where he had entered, he ran all the way back to the camp of the Lorrainers.

Bohemund was already with Godfrey. Although the two stood outside the embroidered and jewel-studded tent which had so lately been a bone of contention, Bohemund was all smiles.

"One of my scouts has brought word that there is a Persian army coming to the relief of Antioch," he said. "It's my feeling that if we were to attack now, the city would fall."

Lord Godfrey regarded him with a puzzled frown. "We have besieged Antioch without success for seven months. What makes you think it would fall now?"

Bohemund smiled innocently. "Somewhere inside there must be a greedy creature who would sell us the privilege of scaling those walls without resistance. I'll undertake to hunt him out."

"And what would be your price?"

The big Norman's face flushed, but he answered quietly enough, "No price. It's understood among all of us that the first one to affix his gonfalon to the ramparts will be the ruler. I'd like my chance along with the rest of you."

Godfrey studied the prince for a long moment. Then he turned suddenly away. "This is a question for all the leaders to decide. Bennet, tell Jacques to sound the signal for a council!"

The boy ran quickly on his errand, and the oliphants were still bouncing their command around the wall when he was back again. Bohemund and Godfrey stood apart from one another, their powerful arms folded, their feet wide spread as if they were balanced for combat. Bohemund's red tunic was torn and dirty. Godfrey's blue was only a little better.

"Master, I have a clean shirt for you," Bennet said quietly.

Godfrey glanced at him with impatience over such a trifle. Then, catching the entreaty in the boy's face, he strode into the tent and stood waiting with an air of expectancy.

Hastily Bennet recounted the incident in the woods.

"So this is why our brother-in-arms has the sudden idea that Antioch will fall!" Godfrey said thoughtfully. "Tell no one of this, boy. We'll do a little plotting of our own!" And he turned to go out again.

"You came in for a clean shirt, my lord," Bennet reminded him, and held out the one Hughette had washed in the river and mended with a thorn for a needle and ravelings for thread.

"Lad, you'd make a good spy, you remember little things," Godfrey laughed, and he rumpled Bennet's hair. The boy was so happy he nearly dropped the shirt.

The council, meeting outside the new tent, listened with varying reactions to Bohemund's crafty proposition. One after the other of the leaders questioned and then agreed to it. Lord Godfrey was among the last. Raymond held out stubbornly against what he called treachery, but everyone knew the real reason was that he would not pass Antioch over to Bohemund. The big Norman, smoothly respectful, did not push his plan.

But by evening a great uneasiness was drawing men into low-voiced groups while the women gathered around the campfires. Kerbogha, Sultan of Mossoul, had collected an army of ten thousand from the banks of the Tigris and the Euphrates and was marching to the relief of Antioch. No one knew exactly how the rumor had started nor why everyone seemed to feel that the Prince of Tarentum could save the day; but Bohemund's name was in every mouth that night. And in the morning Old Barb came loping back from the mountains with the word that Kerbogha was indeed on the way and less than seven days' march from Antioch. Sentiment for Bohemund grew stronger than ever.

In the afternoon Bennet went early to the laurel thickets. Ants ran over him and grasshoppers alighted with thorny feet on his face, but he kept his long vigil. His reward was a piece of news for Lord Godfrey.

"Something has happened to make Phirous afraid to wait, Sire," he told his master in the privacy of the tent. "He thinks Accien suspects him of treason and is going to execute him. So they'll have to move tonight."

With this information Godfrey joined the meeting outside on the carpet. Bohemund reported that he had found a traitor he could trust. Raymond still objected but the others overrode him. The army, they decided, should appear to march away, then return very quietly to their former stand under the walls. The night promised to be dark and stormy, perfect for their purpose. Bohemund, at the Bridge Gate, would ascend the wall by the aid of his friend inside and throw open the little gate. It all sounded very simple.

At sunset the crusaders, with provisions piled hastily into the carts, withdrew in a flutter of flags and trumpet calls. If Accien looked out from his citadel he must surely have believed that the hateful Westerners were finally giving up. Two miles away from the city a halt was made, the women and children were left with a guard, and the fighting men turned as silently as possible back toward the campground they had left. The wind was rising and thunder rumbled in the east, a good cover for the thump of the horses' feet. Suddenly a ball of fire with a long tail appeared in the heavens. All the crusaders who were not mounted fell on their knees.

"A comet," Bennet heard Godfrey say softly, and Bishop Adhemar reply, "A sign from God that we shall take Antioch!"

They were on the narrow length of road between the Bridge Gate and the river, with the great body of the army on the far bank. The wall hulked thirty feet above them, the towers thirty feet more above the wall. There was no way to tell in which of the towers Phirous waited. Not a spark of light showed anywhere.

Bohemund returned from an exploration of the wall. He was so tall his head appeared to brush the low clouds when the lightning flashed.

"There is a leather ladder dangling beside the big gate," he said. "Who will mount with me?"

No one replied.

"Where are my men? Give me some volunteers!"

Still no one came forward, but a voice was heard to grumble that this could be a trap. The traitor might not be such a traitor after all. He could be luring the crusaders to their death.

It was Bohemund's way to roar when he was thwarted, but now he had to keep his voice low. Angrily he harangued his men.

Godfrey whispered close to Bennet's ear. "Now is the time, boy! But if you don't choose to do it, I'll think none the less of you. It's dangerous!"

Bennet felt the chills run down his spine. He knew what Master Godfrey meant. They had worked out their scheme in the afternoon.

"I'm on my way, Sire. Watch for me at the little gate!"

The argument with Bohemund was going on so heatedly that even in the lightning flashes nobody noticed a boy crawling up the ladder. The thing was flimsy. Bennet's hands were skinned and his toes numb before he reached the top. He wormed over the ledge and a hand fell instantly on his shoulder.

"Who are you?" demanded the voice he had heard in the woods.

He couldn't see the fellow well, but he could smell him.

"I'm to open the little gate," Bennet whispered truthfully. "Where is the guard?"

"Dead. It was my brother and I killed him."

"Show me where to go."

"Isn't Bohemund coming up the ladder?"

"It would break under his weight. Where is the gate?"

Phirous led the way to a small stairway of stone leading down into pitch blackness.

"Down there. I let down all the bars but one. You'll find it."

Bennet, remembering Lord Godfrey's caution, descended the steps carefully, backward, his hands on every step. There could be rats and lizards to step on, loose stones to set bouncing to break a bone. But he made the descent safely. At the bottom of the stairs, as Phirous had said, was the heavy iron bar which must hold shut the little gate.

The bar grew slippery with blood from his skinned hands before Bennet felt it give and the gate swung open. Bohemund's men had started finally in a swarm up the ladder and the leather thongs had broken. In the confusion Godfrey's entrance through the little gate went unnoticed.

"Watch for the stairs, Master!" Bennet warned, but already Godfrey was scrambling upward. In the ramparts, he leaped to the edge of the wall, and the boy saw him like a black cut-out figure against the wild sky.

"In at the gate, you men of Lorraine!" he shouted, and the cry rang to the mountains. "Antioch is ours! It is the will of God!"

The cry was taken up as it had been at Clermont and Doryleum and Nicaea, and if Bohemund let out a roar of complaint it went unheard. Men swarmed in at the gate and became a bobbing horde in the streets. People, awakened by the clamor, rushed out of the houses and in the disorder it was impossible to tell which were Christians to be rescued or Turks to be slaughtered. Crowds fought their way to the citadel, others tried to escape through the blocked gates, some took refuge in the churches and mosques.

When dawn finally came, Bohemund's black gonfalon fluttered from one of the highest towers in the city. It made no difference that Godfrey had been first on the wall, the Prince of Tarentum declared in contradiction of his former stand. Antioch would be governed by the one whose cleverness had brought about its downfall. In the joyfulness and excitement of uncovering the riches of the city, no one bothered to dispute him.

For three days in this June of 1098 the crusaders rejoiced, overlooking the fact that the citadel had not been taken and that Kerbogha was tramping stolidly up from the Euphrates with ten thousand men. Kerbogha was not playing at war. He was a lifetime warrior, and under him were the sultans of Nicaea, Aleppo, and Damascus, the governor of Jerusalem, and twenty emirs from Persia, Palestine, and Syria. On the sixth of June his tents blossomed like pointed toadstools on the west bank of the Orontes and to the north of the road to Aleppo. And the crusaders were caught between the force at the citadel and the enemy outside the walls.

Old Barb, making a circuit of the enemy camp, reported that Kerbogha had taken over the Port of St. Simeon, thus cutting off the food supply. It would be only a matter of time until famine would deliver the Army of the West into the hands of the Turks.

Help would have arrived except for the action of Count Stephen of Blois. Deserting with a great number of his followers, he marched north and met Alexius who was coming south with a large Greek army as well as a body of crusaders who had arrived late. The cause was lost, Stephen

declared. Alexius did not want to match strategy with Kerbogha. Breaking camp as if the fierce warrior already nipped
at his heels, he returned to Constantinople.

Every form of suffering now descended upon the crusaders
cooped up within the walls. The small river was insufficient
for thousands of thirsty men and horses, and soon it became
a muddy course steaming in the summer heat. The once
beautiful orchards were stripped of leaves by the starving
animals which in turn were killed and eaten by the famished
people. A loaf of bread sold for a bezant; then there was no
bread to be had at any price. Lord Godfrey, trying in vain
to encourage his people, heard them blaspheme the God
who had led them into this heathen land and could give
them no answer. He could not feed them any more. His
last war horse had been butchered and eaten. Every night
more deserters crawled over the walls by means of rope
ladders, which earned them the name of rope dancers, and
escaped into the mountains. Bohemund was wounded by an
arrow from the citadel and became so ill that the priests
prayed night and day beside him. Women screamed to the
Blessed Virgin that she, who had borne a son, should take
pity on their children. The children were too weak to cry,
the living too weak to bury the dead. At the end of two
weeks a truce was asked of Kerbogha whereby he would
give safe passage out of the city and permit them to return
to their own countries, but the sultan only laughed.

That was why, when a hitherto unknown young priest
named Peter Bartholomew revealed that he had had a most
remarkable dream, the few devout took up his cause instantly
and the scoffers dared to hope. Nothing but a miracle, it
appeared, could save the crusaders. And the miracle, according to Peter, was about to happen.

CHAPTER ELEVEN
THE HOLY LANCE

"Not only once did I dream, but three times!" Peter Bartholomew cried. "Three times the same dream! St. Andrew appeared to me in a flaming cloud and cried out, 'Go to the church of my brother Peter and dig up the earth before the main altar. There you will find the iron head of the lance which pierced the side of our Redeemer. Carry this lance head before the army and it will pierce the hearts of the infidels!'"

Peter stopped for breath. He was not unlike Peter the Hermit, Bennet thought as he watched him. Much younger, but just as thin and ragged, and with the same fierce devotion burning in his dark face. Around him the company had gathered, most of them seated weakly on the edge of the huge empty crater which had been the pool of the public bath. There was Bohemund, gaunt and lying sideways to ease the pressure on his sore leg; Godfrey pallid under his sunburn, Hugh arrayed in a purple robe he had taken from a Greek and still wearing the emperor's costly bracelets clear to his shoulders. Raymond was grizzled and muscular as ever. Young Tancred had the bleached look of starvation, his blond hair no longer fashionably short but hanging now to his shoulders.

"So God has not forgotten us," Tancred said softly. "We'll reach Jerusalem! As long as I have sixty companions left, I'll break out of here and get to Jerusalem!"

"Amen!" said Raymond, and Godfrey nodded.

"God bless you," Bishop Adhemar breathed. He was weak and sick, as pale as the marble pillar he leaned against.

Bennet, being only a squire, could say nothing, but in his heart he also took the oath. He wouldn't need sixty companions. With Godfrey, or Tancred alone, he would go on until he saw the Holy City. A handful of pilgrims could not rescue Jerusalem, but they could offer their efforts as a prayer for more aid. God surely would listen to men who spoke to Him from His own city.

"Where do we dig, Peter?" Tancred asked.

But Peter held up his hand. "We must pray and fast for three days first."

Godfrey's smile was somewhat ironic. "The fasting will be no problem."

"Don't ridicule him," the bishop cautioned. "There will

be others to do that. Sound the oliphants for a gathering of the people in the churches. Peter and I will visit all of them and announce this grace of God."

Many others, as the bishop warned, did sneer at Peter's dream. But among the fervent believers was Peter the Hermit. He had remained very quiet. Now he took up Peter Bartholomew's cause and preached in his old feverish style. Enthusiasm boiled up to such a pitch that the watching armies of Kerbogha were treated to the strange sight of women and children marching in processions on top of the wide wall, singing and praying. On the morning of the third day a group of twelve including Godfrey, Raymond, Peter Bartholomew, Bishop Adhemar, Tancred, and Ku-ku Peter entered the Church of St. Peter and knelt long in prayer. Then, calling forward the workmen who had come with them, they took the tools to pry up the stones forming the floor before the altar.

Bennet, staying quietly in the back of the church, watched breathlessly. The work was slow. The knights had been magnificent athletes when they set out from Constantinople, but now they were scarcely able to stand. Four of them panted over the work of one. But the stones came up and the picks bit into the earth underneath. Now, the watchers whispered to one another, any minute the spades would strike the holy iron. But the hours went by and the hole grew larger and there was no sound of metal striking metal.

At twilight the work ceased. At midnight, because this was their only hope, the same men came back and began to dig again by the light of flares held by the squires. Standing in a circle around the deep, wide hole, those who were not working began to pray. The spectators joined. The sound of the praying rolled through the locked and guarded door and out to the people who reclined in the streets, too weak to stand through their vigil. The sound increased until it seemed to vibrate against the big low stars, and Kerbogha's men outside the walls heard it with strange uneasiness. The Christians' prayers were disturbing, and the warriors gripped their lances while they assured themselves that all the praying in the world could avail nothing to this surrounded, starving enemy.

In the church the men finally threw down the shovels. Godfrey nearly knocked the flare out of Bennet's hand as he turned on Peter Bartholomew.

"You and your dreams! What have they brought us but a waste of time and strength!"

"God will not let it be so!" Peter cried. "Give me a spade!"

Snatching a spade from a workman, he leaped into the hole some twelve feet deep by now. Bennet leaned over, holding his flare to light the black abyss. Peter dug frantically. Suddenly he fell to his knees, tearing at the earth with his hands.

"The lance!" he cried, and sprang up with a darkly wrapped thing held high into the light of the torches.

Bishop Adhemar, kneeling, stretched out his hands and Peter laid the object in them. The wrapping was very old, some kind of silk darkened by age and the earth. It fell away to disclose a deeply rusted, pointed head of a lance.

The men dropped to their knees, a circle of spellbound faces ringed by the flaring torches.

"The lance is found!" a squire cried at the back of the church.

The cry slipped through the locked door out into the street, to be taken up and flung through the city until it spilled out over the wall. The Turkish warriors leaped to arms because this cry of exultation was even more disturbing than the praying had been. The sounds of rejoicing went on all night, and at dawn the Angelus was rung by bells which had called the infidels to worship.

The bells had barely died to silence when the small gate beside the bridge opened and Ku-ku Peter, barefooted and ragged and tousled of head, rode out on his mule. He was alone and he was bound for the camp of Kerbogha with a message. If the Turks wished to retreat and return to their own country, he told the sultan, the Christians would guarantee them safe conduct. The princes would even instruct their people to pray that the infidels' eyes might be opened to the true faith. But if they were unwilling to accept the blessings of peace, then the Christians would engage them in such a battle as would show the justice of their cause.

Kerbogha, in the magnificence of his scarlet tent, surrounded by warriors with ready swords and worn tempers, was enraged at this piece of impudence. He leaped up on his stocky legs and shook his fist in Peter's face, trembling from his gold helmet down to his gold-slippered feet.

"Go back and tell the dogs that I am the conqueror and it is my place to dictate conditions, not receive them! If they will acknowledge Mahomet as their god, then I might forget their insolence. But they must do so today! Tomorrow we will put the sword to them! Their God could not save Himself from the cross and He will not save them from the sword of Kerbogha!"

And he whipped out his scimitar and cut the air above Peter's head. The hermit beat a hasty retreat and nearly lost his life several times on the way back into the city.

The answer was what the leaders had expected. Even while Peter was gone, preparations for battle had been going on. A small store of provisions had been found, seemingly by a miracle, and there was a skimpy meal for those who must fight. Then the soldiers crowded into the churches where they prayed all through the night.

On the morning of June 29, the feast of Sts. Peter and Paul, the stones were rolled away from the gates and the army marched out in twelve divisions symbolic of the twelve apostles. Each leader was at the head of his own men. Before them all rode Bishop Adhemar bearing the Holy Lance, and with him holding the yellow and white standard of the Church was Hugh the Great. Only Raymond remained behind within the walls to watch the garrison in the citadel. From the top of the wall the priests blessed the passing armies while the women and children sang. Bennet, on foot beside his master who rode a borrowed horse, saw Hughette wave to him. He knew he did not look like a knight or even a squire in his tattered hose and his hauberk with half the links gone—but he had a lady on the ramparts! She would be praying for him.

Kerbogha, looking down with his battalions from the neighboring hills, saw how the foot soldiers tottered with weakness and how the knights and barons rode donkeys or camels or walked with the soldiers. But he saw also that, staggering though they were, they marched straight forward. The warrior could not help admiring this last stand of a gallant people, and so he permitted them to take their time westward until they came to the spot where the mountains sweep down to the Orontes. There, backed by the natural defense of the mountains, they ranged themselves for battle. Hugh, with the Church standard, took the left wing with Godfrey at the right and the bishop in the center. Bohemund remained at a distance where he could watch the battle and rush his reserves to wherever they were needed. On the vast plain there was no sound but the quiet voices of the leaders and the chant of Adhemar, "Let the Lord arise and

let His enemies be dispersed!" A few birds even flew up
singing out of the meadow grass.

Kerbogha on his hill looked down with sudden fear at
this quiet assemblage. He never had prayed, going into
battle, but had sent his armies forward savagely with bleat-
ing trumpets and racketing drums. Up the Orontes the
sultans of Nicaea, Damascus, and Aleppo had wedged themselves in between the Christians and the city. Fifteen divisions, well fed and thirsting for battle, were ready to meet
the half-starved army of the West. Yet Kerbogha took a
last look at Bohemund's black gonfalon hoisted on the wall
of Antioch and did something he never had done before.
He sent an emissary to suggest that the Christians select
fifty of their finest knights to fight fifty of his picked men
and thus save bloodshed on both sides.

Under the standard held by Hugh the leaders came together to receive the messenger.

"No," Godfrey said shortly. "God has given us too many
signs of His favor today, even a strong wind at our backs
to speed our lances and hold back their arrows. No, we'll
wait only for the messenger to regain his own lines and then
we'll attack!"

But Kerbogha, caring nothing for the safety of one man,
saw the white flag start reluctantly back and gave the order
to rush the lines. Screaming, on plunging horses, the Turks
dashed forward in a hail of arrows.

"My lance!" Godfrey cried, and Bennet had only time to
thrust it into his hand before the wildly shouting enemy was
upon them.

The squires, who could not bear arms, were supposed to
watch the fighting from a safe distance. Bennet scrambled
to the top of a small knoll. Later he would know that the
Sultan of Nicaea, coming up the Orontes, fell heavily upon

Bohemund at the same time that the sons of Accien charged Godfrey and the Sword of the Lion flew down from the hills upon Hugh and Tancred. The crusaders fought desperately, but the Turks had learned from them the skill of hand-to-hand fighting and by sheer numbers they pushed the lines back across the plains and up the first low ascent of the mountains. The Sultan of Nicaea ordered flaming flax to be pitched into the low bushes and dried grass, and now the friendly wind became an enemy to carry forward smoke and sparks. In the thick, choking cloud the ranks of the crusaders broke. All that was left was for the sultan to rush in and snatch the standard from Hugh to claim his victory.

And then, suddenly, on the mountains high above the wavering ranks of the crusaders three horsemen appeared. The squires on the knoll saw them first. They were mounted on white horses and they wore snow-white mail with white-bannered lances held in the martial position, the staff resting in the left stirrup and the left arm pointing the lance straight ahead. The visors were down on the helmets, hiding the faces of the knights. As if a miraculous draft breathed down upon it, the smoke receded to earth so that now all the thousands of knights and warriors could see over it. Utterly motionless, the strange mailed figures sat their horses on the rocky eminence. Even the wounded were silent while those unearthly, faceless knights held their position.

"They are saints!" Bishop Adhemar cried, and such was the quiet that his voice carried far over the multitude. "St. George the Great Martyr, St. Demetrius, and St. Theodore! They have come to lead us! *It is the will of God!*"

"It is the will of God!" the army took up the cry.

The Turks had heard that battle signal before and it struck fear into them. Pushing ahead of the flames, the crusaders fought like demented men. The standard of Bouillon had gone down and beside it Lord Godfrey, unhorsed, fought desperately with three assailants. Bennet leaped down from the boulder where he had sat and ran to his master's defense. Yanking a scimitar from the hand of a dead Turk, he slashed as fiercely as any soldier of the sultan. Jacques, wounded, lay on top of the gonfalon. The army would waver in their attack unless they could see the banner. Pushing Jacques aside, Bennet raised the blue aloft again and a cheer answered him. All over the field now, standards were being raised. The Turks in a mighty rout were galloping into the mountains, leaving behind them the provisions which would be as precious as the victory. At the same time, back in the citadel, the lookouts saw the rout and were so terrified that the entire garrison surrendered to Raymond without an arrow being shot.

That night, in the Church of St. Peter where the burial place of the lance was still a gaping hole, Bishop Adhemar sang a *Te Deum;* but the church was half empty. The crusaders, victorious, were out on the plains arguing over who should have custody of the marvelous tent of Kerbogha. The tent could hold two thousand people and was studded with precious gems and leafed with gold, and the corridors splitting its vast area into rooms were all laid with carpet and white goatskins.

"Let us go on to Jerusalem immediately," the bishop pleaded with the men. "The governor of Jerusalem fled before us today, he'll give us no resistance. Christ pleads that we rescue His tomb. Move on tomorrow!"

"We have beaten the Turks too often for us to fear them now," Eustace said. "We're exhausted by starvation. Now that we have supplies, let's rest and regain our health through the heat of summer. Reinforcements are on the way from home. When they've reached us, then we'll march on to Jerusalem."

"Push the victory to the finish!" Bohemund argued. "We'll make Antioch into a Christian city and then to Jerusalem."

"Leaving you behind as governor, of course?" Raymond sneered.

"Why not? I was first over the wall!"

"Godfrey was first!"

"Let Bohemund stay if he wishes," Godfrey said wearily. "I swore to bring aid to the Christians of Jerusalem and I'll do it!"

The wrangling went on through the hot summer days. Pestilence soon filtered into the city and death reigned there more terribly than on the battlefield. Bishop Adhemar sickened among the first and was buried in the very place where they had dug up the lance. Without his firm spiritual leadership the crusaders divided into factions, and even the lance which had been proclaimed miraculous was now an object of controversy. Peter Bartholomew, his enemies said, had found the iron head somewhere on the march and slipped it into the church inside his tunic. Peter's defenders spoke up for him staunchly, and there were many fist fights in the old streets.

Provisions ran so low that again there were thirst and famine, and every day a few deserters straggled out across the plains in search of towns to plunder. Word came that Hugh the Great, who had gone back to Constantinople to implore aid from Alexius, had become disconsolate over the refusal of the emperor and had embarked with all of his men for Europe. Raymond, declaring that he could no longer tolerate the company of Bohemund, laid siege to the city of Maarah. No sooner had he conquered it than Bohemund arrived to claim half the spoils, which amounted to little since Raymond had burned it to the ground and sold the inhabitants into slavery. Others of the nobles, inspired by Raymond's success, marched against smaller cities which surrendered without a battle, for so terrible had the reputation of the crusaders become that it was said women were killing their own children rather than have them fall into the hands of the Westerners.

Sickened and revolted by the greediness of their leaders, the people finally rebelled. Raymond's men opened the gates of Maarah and headed back to Antioch, and the old warrior, to save face, was forced to pretend he had only been waiting for the will of his people to lead the return. Back in the city by the Orontes he saw that Tancred, taking advantage of his absence, had hoisted Bohemund's black gonfalon on the battered wall of the citadel.

Again the princes were at one another's throats while the famished, sick, thirsty people wondered when, if ever, the noblemen would remember why they had come on crusade at all.

CHAPTER TWELVE
THE ORDEAL OF FIRE

Once again the Army of the West was reassembled in the city beside the Orontes. Gathered in the market place where the old odors of sesame and spices still lingered in the booths around the open square, they did not look like an army. The men who had broken out of Maarah were even more emaciated than those who had remained in Antioch. All were ragged and starved, many were sick.

But it was Christmas morning of 1098, and there had been visions through the night of the dead warriors returning to hearten their brothers, especially Bishop Adhemar who wept over the discord. As many as could crowd into the Church of St. Peter had heard the Mass said over the very spot where the bishop lay buried, and now in the market they had come together with a purpose.

Fulcher of Chartres, a priest who was keeping a careful journal of all the happenings of the crusade, had been chosen as speaker. In rags, barefooted, he stood on the stone block from which slaves had been auctioned. Before him in a small body were the princes who were still the leaders—Bohemund with his enormous arms folded across his mighty chest, Tancred at a distance from him because he was finally tiring of his uncle's stubborn greed, Godfrey pale and anxious, Raymond peering suspiciously with his one eye. Back from this small group, separated by a wall of hostility, was the throng of crusaders.

Bennet, perched at the foot of a marble column, looked around at the camels and the flat-roofed white houses ranking up the hills and the miserable people clothed in the strange, borrowed robes of the East, and he thought of that other Christmas morning back at Bouillon when he had been so ashamed of his father for not taking the cross. Unless something could be done immediately to break the deadlock among the leaders, Papa's prophecy would come true. The crusade would fall in its own tracks.

"Two years ago today," said Fulcher, "I took the cross in Chartres. Jerusalem did not seem so far away. A year ago today we were in Constantinople, on the threshold of the Holy Land, and again Jerusalem was near. But now, on this third Christmas, it seems to us that our leaders have forgotten why we left our homes and our loved ones. Five months ago we took this city. Why have we not gone on? From the borders of Hungary to Nicaea and the plains before Antioch we have left our dead. Did we do this to gain the governor's chair of a pagan city for one prince, or did we do it to ransom the tomb of Jesus Christ?" Fulcher stepped to the very edge of the block. "We, the followers, are not remaining any longer in Antioch. If you wish to stay, Sires, then we will choose from among us a knight we can trust and we will go on to Jerusalem with him as our leader!"

A great cheer broke from the people. Bennet watched Lord Godfrey. On the battlefield he could lead a charge with inspired courage. But now he stood with his eyes cast down to the cobblestones and said nothing.

"Why doesn't he speak?" Gareau groaned. "The people are begging him for leadership! Why can't he give it to them?"

Bennet's fists doubled, and the troubadour smiled faintly. "Don't peck me, bantam rooster! You know as well as I do that this whole crusade has been held together only by faith."

"Which proves that God is our leader," said a priest who stood nearby. "We need no other. Perhaps God will send us on now without our princes."

Old Raymond stepped forward. "I don't think it prudent to march yet——" He had to pause until a wave of booing died away. Then he went on firmly, "I don't think it wise, but I bow to your will. Let's first make an expedition into the country around and gather what provisions we can. Then we'll march to Arkas."

"Why Arkas?" someone asked. "Why not Jerusalem?"

"Because we must conquer each city we approach or we'll leave the enemy free to follow us!"

"I'll go with you," Bohemund said.

Raymond whirled on him. "Arkas will be mine!"

Godfrey, his face dark with anger, strode forward in front of them all. "I agree that we've lost sight of our holy purpose at times, but caution must not be mistaken for faintheartedness. I'll push straight to Jerusalem, but not tomorrow! How far would we get in the winter rains? Where would we find food for ourselves and our horses?"

A camel sneezed, someone called, "What horses?" and the people laughed.

"Divide then!" Raymond cried. "All you who want to push on, come with me. The others stay here with Duke Godfrey. For myself, I'll pay well any other leader who will join me."

"I'll go!" Tancred shouted, and there was a loud agreement among the young knights.

"Godfrey is right," Gareau said, watching the people breaking into groups. "Raymond will bog down at Arkas, and he and Bohemund will be fighting in the mud. We'll catch up with them there in the spring."

"My master is always right!" Bennet declared, and Gareau smiled, shrugging.

In May of 1099 Godfrey's band finally marched out through the Bridge Gate. Bohemund made a show of leaving the city but soon turned back to install himself as governor of Antioch. Reaching Laodicea, Godfrey liberated some Flemish pirates who had been kept prisoner by the Greeks for more than a year, and he was joined by new crusaders from Holland, Flanders, and England. Then, with the white rock cliffs of Lebanon towering ten thousand feet on their left and the eternal blue of the Mediterranean on their right, the army moved south through olive orchards and fields rich with corn.

At Arkas, as Gareau had predicted, they came upon

Raymond stubbornly besieging a city which just as stubbornly held out against him. His followers had stripped the land of everything edible and were once again on the edge of famine. In their extremity the people who had come so far on this mission of faith now lost faith and hope, and Peter Bartholomew became the target for their complaints against God. The lance had once been the symbol of God's leadership. Peter had carried it with Raymond to Arkas. Now it had become a point of division.

Since Godfrey had not been present during the rising discord, the problem was laid before him as mediator on his first day in camp. They ranged themselves on the hillside, the Normans from the north of France in one faction, the southerners from Toulouse in the other since Peter Bartholomew was one of Count Raymond's chaplains. Between them stood Peter, so emaciated now that he could have passed for the twin of Peter the Hermit.

Bennet, holding the blue gonfalon behind Lord Godfrey's chair, saw the group of tattered, hungry men with the scarred wall of Arkas pointing the horizon behind them. There were almost no tents pitched on the hillsides. The people lay in the burning sunlight, a horde of beggars snarling and quarreling. In their bickering over the lance they had forgotten their dream of Jerusalem.

"Why must you take sides?" Lord Godfrey asked. "Why can't each one believe as he likes about the holiness of the lance?"

Angry murmurs began on both sides, and Peter answered quickly, "Sire, the lance has become a wedge to divide us. Since I was the one who found it, I must be the one to prove its truth. There is but one way. The ordeal of fire!"

Even the Normans cringed, and Godfrey said, "No, Peter! That will not be required of you."

"I offer myself freely! God will preserve me! I'll carry the lance through living fire and come out untouched!"

"I'll not permit it," Raymond declared.

But Arnold, the speaker for the Normans, had a louder voice. "Let him make the test! If this is the lance which pierced Our Lord's side, then it will indeed keep Peter from the flames!"

"Good Friday is three days away," Peter said. "Build me a pyre of olive branches and on the day of Christ's supreme sacrifice I'll prove the miraculous power of the lance!"

"Agreed!" shouted Arnold.

"No!" Godfrey cried. But he was outshouted.

Apparently forgetting that they had agreed to abide by the duke's decision as mediator, Peter's friends tossed the frail little man to their shoulders and bore him away in a frenzy of enthusiasm. The Normans, satisfied, departed for their camp.

Godfrey and Bennet were left alone before the tattered blue tent.

"I don't like it," Godfrey said wearily. "Our love of God alone should keep us united. He may well have lost patience with all our squabbling and will refuse to grant us a miracle to bring us together."

"Then, Sire, even if the lance is real, Peter may be burned?" Bennet asked.

"I'm afraid so. Look at us, Bennet. . . ." He gestured toward the camp. "Are we praying, offering our suffering to God as the price of our victory in Jerusalem? Oh, no, we are going to tempt His justice by demanding a sign from Him when we should be down on our knees thanking Him for sparing us thus far! We in ourselves deserve nothing. Our only worth is in what we can accomplish for Him. And still, here we lie, wasting our last bit of strength in a quarrel over whose human judgment is right!"

Godfrey dropped his head into his hands. Bennet was a little frightened. He never had heard his master speak like this before. In silence he rolled the gonfalon carefully around the staff and tied it with the tattered ribbons. Even with all the devotion Jacques gave it, the blue banner might not outlast the long delays. Whose gonfalon, then, would fly from the wall of Jerusalem? And would Godfrey be there? Each day he lost a little more weight, became a little more tired. Tonight he would eat even less than his people because he always insisted on giving away any morsel he had. In the pot Hughette was tending there was but a handful of the bitter leaves of the burdock.

By Friday, out on the great plain, a towering pyre of olive branches with an aisle through the middle barely two feet wide had been erected. Through that narrow aisle topped no higher than his head, Peter Bartholomew must pass. The flames would roar around him and above him. The entire army of pilgrims was out on the plain to watch the ordeal. At the place where Peter would enter the flames were Raymond and Arnold, Godfrey and Robert of Flanders and the other princes. On the opposite side of the pyre, where Peter must come out, the sick were gathered to touch the lance after the miracle had taken place.

Bennet had gone so early to the site that he had a position immediately behind the sick who lay on the ground. As the hour drew near, like everyone else he trembled with excitement. All eyes were fastened on the small brush shelter a short distance off in which Peter was preparing himself. Clergy in vestments they had carried from France surrounded the shelter and made an avenue to the pyre. At exactly three o'clock Peter came out of the shelter. He wore only a white tunic and in his hands, uplifted, was the darkly rusted head of the lance.

The crowd had not been noisy before, but now it was utterly silent. Peter stopped before the Bishop of Albara who intoned loudly.

"If this man has truly seen Jesus Christ in a vision, and if the Apostle Andrew did reveal to him the hidingplace of the divine lance, then may he come untouched through the flames. But if he has not spoken truly as to his visions and the lance, then may the flames devour him!"

"It is the will of God!" the priests chanted.

Peter fell on his knees and kissed the hem of the bishop's cassock. "As God is my witness, I have not lied! I will not be touched by the fire!" Then, rising and holding the lance high, he cried to the people, "Pray for me!"

The smoke began to rise from the brush heap. When it was entirely in flames, Peter started slowly forward. Bennet lost sight of him as he neared the pyre. The heat was so intense that the sick people were turning their backs. Bennet held his hands before his face, but through his fingers he watched the small opening where the smoke billowed and the flames were beginning to lick. How could Peter find his way inside?

"He'll die, he'll die," Bennet groaned, not realizing that he had spoken aloud until Old Barb answered.

"Don't look, boy."

"I have to! Where is he?"

"Burned up!"

"Oh, no, no . . ."

But far too much time had elapsed. A woman screamed, many were weeping and moaning.

And then, suddenly, Peter burst forth, the lance still in his hands, his eyes red from smoke and most of his tunic burned away. His skin had been browned by the sun to the color of a ripe nut, but so far as Bennet could see there were no marks from the fire. The lance was untouched.

"A miracle!" someone shouted, and immediately the shout was taken up until it ran like a wind over the plain.

A sick man pushed himself near to Peter and caught at the rag of his tunic. As if that were the signal, the crowd rushed at the little man. The sick were trampled and shoved aside, and Peter's cries were lost in the wild tumult. Even the Normans joined in the mad scramble to embrace this priest whose vision was now known to be authentic.

Bennet fought his way out of the mob and joined Lord Godfrey who stood by himself back on the plain.

"The miracle has happened, Sire!" the boy cried.

But Godfrey said, "I wonder."

And three days later, Peter died.

CHAPTER THIRTEEN
BETHLEHEM

"So Peter Bartholomew's sacrifice has accomplished nothing," Gareau said. "We couldn't agree on whether the lance was miraculous. Now we can't agree on Peter's death. Did he come through the flames untouched, only to be killed by the too eager embraces of his followers? Or did the fire burn him?" He slapped the neck of the bronze lion upon which he sat. "Nobody ever will know."

Bennet, lolling on the steps of the sunken garden, looked down at the empty marble basin of the fountain. A few leaves blew across it in the dry wind. Three days had gone by since the burial of Peter and still the leaders argued in the great deserted palace outside the walls of Arkas. Raymond insisted that the city must fall; most of the others were in favor of going on. Through the high windows of the hall flanking the garden their voices drifted to the two beside the fountain.

"Around and around," Gareau added, "like pups chasing one another around a dead tree. Who's winning?"

"Does it matter, as long as we get to Jerusalem?"

"Not a whit, young sir. But *when* do we get to Jerusalem?"

The voices were rising inside the hall, and the two turned, listening. Words could not be distinguished, but Bohemund's full-throated roar was the core of all the wrangling.

Gareau, astride the lion, wheeled his back toward the hall. "Why can't Godfrey speak up? He could lead if he would! On the battlefield he's magnificent, the knights follow him anywhere! Where is his tongue now?"

Bennet leaped up. He wore only a length of linen wrapped about his brown body, perfect garb for a fighter. In one swift lunge he pushed Gareau off the lion and the two rolled battling down the steps and into the dry basin.

Bennet pounded away at the troubadour, releasing all the fury of his own disappointment in Lord Godfrey, his hunger and thirst and terrible discontent through the long months since Constantinople. He did not know there was an observer until a firm voice spoke.

"Boy! What does this mean?"

Bennet, astride Gareau, left off his thumping of the troubadour's head against the marble and looked up. Lord Godfrey stood at the top of the steps, magnificently tall against the blue sky, brown hair lying on his bronzed shoulders above the white linen toga. The boy sprang to his feet and Gareau got up painfully, brushing off leaves. Godfrey did not insist on an answer to his question. In his gray eyes there was understanding.

"We'll be too busy for quarreling, Bennet. Tomorrow morning we move out of Arkas." He glanced from the squire to the troubadour as if he could read all that had gone on. "Nothing will keep us from Jerusalem now!"

Turning, the Lord of Bouillon strode off through the garden with new life in his step. Solemnly Bennet and Gareau shook hands.

The next morning, as Godfrey had promised, the army marched away with trumpets calling and the blue gonfalon spreading its tatters on the wind. Tancred and most of Raymond's men went with them. By noon the Count of Toulouse could see even with his one eye that he would be left alone under the walls of Arkas, and he spurred his horse to catch up with the rest of the army.

The people were overjoyed. Marching through Phoenicia they found that the harvest was done and provisions plentiful. The twenty-mile-wide strip between the mountains of Lebanon and the sea was thick with olive trees tall as elms and pomegranates with red and yellow fruit big as a man's fist. Oranges, a fruit the Europeans never had seen, littered the ground and a tall reedy plant, called sugar cane by the natives, was sweet to cut and suck. In the earlier days when the army had come into a land of plenty there had been much waste and gluttony. By now the once gluttonous ones had died of starvation, those who worshipped wealth enough to be wasteful had stayed behind in Edessa and Antioch, and the weak had returned home or lay in graves without markings. Of the fifty thousand strong who had moved out of Europe, barely five thousand remained, but these were the cream risen above all hardships. They could fast without starving, withstand the burning sun and the choking dust and the sweat scalding them under the armor. They could look toward Jerusalem and, forgetting the miseries that stretched behind them two years long, see only the vision they had seen beside the home fires in France—service to God through the redemption of the lands where He had walked.

The journey seemed to be blessed by heaven. Small seacoast cities surrendered without even being asked and sent out provisions. Hermits who had taken to the mountains to avoid persecution by the Turks came down to act as guides through the rocky ravines leading to the plain of Berytus. Leaving Jaffa on their right, the columns drew away from the seacoast and took peaceful possession of Lydda, a town deserted by the Turks. Here St. George had been martyred and a beautiful church erected over the place of his death. The Christians were not to see the church, for the Turks set fire to it before moving out.

At Ramlah the army made its last camp. Sixteen miles now from Jerusalem! The expectation and excitement of the people was limitless. Yet once again the princes fell to quarreling.

"If we continue straight to Jerusalem without provisions, we may not be able to carry on the siege long enough to take the city," said Raymond. "But if we go down into Egypt and conquer the sultan, then the riches of Cairo and Alexandria will fall without battle into our hands!"

"And those golden cities must have governors, and who is more anxious to govern than you, Count Raymond?" Eustace demanded.

Bennet, standing behind Lord Godfrey in the blue tent, held his breath for his master's view.

"I wonder if it could be possible that the long way around by Cairo might be the shortest route to Jerusalem?" the duke said musingly. "We need provisions. . . ."

Bennet didn't wait to hear more. Ducking out of the tent he ran into the night where the stars hung like lanterns over the hills just as they had hung on the night that Christ was born. The wind blew from Jerusalem, sweet with the smell of ripe figs and dry with desert dust. He didn't stop running until he was atop a bare foothill and all the camp with its twinkling fires lay below him.

He was not alone on the hill. Hughette was there, seated with her knees drawn up and her hands clasped around them. She had grown taller in the two years since they had left Bouillon. She had seen death and starvation, and now she was a woman.

Bennet threw himself on the grass near her, and for a long time they said nothing. Down in the camp the camels made their complaining whine, a few donkeys brayed and a horse whinnied. There were no dogs to bark since the days of famine in Antioch.

"Lord Godfrey is just like the others," Bennet said finally. "But I won't go down into Egypt with him! If he turns aside now, he'll have to find himself another squire!"

"You'd never become a knight then."

"I don't care!"

Bennet knew that Hughette did not believe him. He didn't believe himself. He still longed to be knighted—by Lord Godfrey—in the Church of the Holy Sepulchre. But even more important to him than the knighthood was the great, compelling dream, as Gareau had called it, which had sent them all so far from home and into a strange land. The Pope had begged at Clermont for aid to the Holy Land. The Christians in Jerusalem must know by now that an army lay only a few miles off. Were their hopes to be killed? And were all the crusaders to lose the dream on the very hills where the shepherds, seeing the star, had turned their feet toward Bethlehem?

The people, however, had no taste for a long side journey into Egypt and at dawn they began to straggle on. The leaders joined them reluctantly, and that night camp was made at Nicopolis, the ancient Emmaus of the Bible. Again there was a council in the blue tent, with Old Barb reporting on what he had seen ahead between Nicopolis and Jerusalem.

"Desert," he said. "The heathens are busy making away with the water supply. Every well and cistern is poisoned, the dams open and the rivers dried up. There's enough to eat, but we'll thirst to death!"

As he had done the night before, Bennet listened tensely for Godfrey's reply; and when it came it was quite as disappointing.

"We number but a few thousand men strong enough to fight. What do you say if we remain here for a few days and consider all things carefully?"

Bennet whirled, ready to dash away again, but Gareau laid his hand on the boy's shoulder.

"Wait! Look at the road."

Along the dusty red road a handful of people were approaching from the direction of Jerusalem. They wore the long garments of the Christians of the East, and behind them the crusaders were flowing into the road to follow. They continued up the slope until they stood before the princes. One, a huge Viking with hair to his shoulders and a shepherd's crook in his hand, stepped forward.

"We came to the Holy Land long ago and have stayed, praying for rescue. Now we come from Bethlehem. The Moslems in the village have heard of your approach and it is their intention to set fire to the beautiful new church we have just built over the Manger!"

Some of the crusaders fell on their knees at the mention of the Holy Place, and Lord Godfrey crossed himself. Surely, Bennet thought, the Master of Bouillon would remember the ruins of the Church of St. George in Lydda and he would take instant action to preserve the Manger.

But when Godfrey spoke, it was to ask about the water supply. There was no suggestion that the army push on, and camp was made as usual for the night.

The duke had retired and Bennet was lying, wide awake, in his usual place before the tent when Hughette slipped out of the shadows.

"They're going to Bethlehem!" she whispered.

"Who?"

"Tancred and about a hundred of the young knights and squires. They're going to take possession before the Moslems can burn the church!"

"Have they left yet?"

"No. They're gathering down the road."

Bennet didn't hesitate. Running down the hill to the valley where the horses had pawed the sand into dunes in their search for water, he leaped on to the first animal he could catch and rode bareback to the place Hughette had indicated.

The young knights wore their full mail except for the helmets which the squires carried. They were very quiet, ghostly in the moonlight. Tancred looked over his company, then gave the word to ride. Once out of hearing of the sleeping camp, they sent their horses at a gallop over the hills toward Bethlehem.

Suddenly the moon darkened and disappeared, and the horses stumbled in the pitch black.

"What now?" the riders asked. "Is this a sign that we should go back?"

"Wait," said Tancred, "and pray while we wait."

So, sitting their horses, the handful of strangers prayed under the stars. The moon at last reappeared, but now her face was blood-red.

"By the grace of God we'll take Jerusalem!" Tancred said softly. "But it will be a bloody siege. On now to Bethlehem!"

At midnight, in the same darkness in which the Child was born in the stable, the young riders entered the old streets. Tancred halted them while his standard-bearer set his gonfalon on the white wall. Then, quiet as raiders, they walked their horses to the church. It was easy to find, a magnificent structure built by the loving hands of the Christians. Inside, lighted by the candle flames bobbing before it, was the dark little grotto in which the Baby had lain.

By the time the newcomers left the church the inhabitants of the town had awakened and ventured at first fearfully into the streets, then with shouts of joy.

"Bethlehem is free! The Moslems are gone!" they cried, and flocked around the riders, pulling some of them down to kiss them. In the general commotion it was not noticed that one of the riders quietly reined his horse into a narrow old street that did not lead back to the Nicopolis Road. Just as quietly, Bennet followed. He knew what Tancred was going to do. Outside the town he caught up and they sent their horses at a gallop over the road Mary had traveled with her Child.

Crossing the Valley of Jehosophat they ascended a hill dark with olive groves. The horses were short of breath by the time they came out on the grassy summit. The hill fell away to the west into a deep ravine, then mounted again into a long slope crowned by a great stone wall. Beyond the wall, small in the distance, were the familiar rounded domes of Turkish mosques rosy in the faint light of dawn.

Sitting his horse beside Tancred, Bennet looked long at the gray stones and the parched hills.

"Jerusalem?"

Tancred smiled. "Jerusalem! We are here!"

"From where have you come?" a voice asked in perfect French.

The two turned, startled. An old man in sackcloth and with a gray beard hanging to his waist was regarding them from only a few steps away.

"I mean no harm," he said. "Who are you?"

"I'm Tancred, a Norman knight. At Nicopolis lies the whole Christian army ready to liberate Jerusalem!"

The old man smiled. "You say it easily. Do you know where you stand now? On the Mount of Olives. Down there at the foot of this mountain runs the brook Kedron, and beside it is the Garden of Gethsemane where Our Lord sweat blood. The Normans will shed much of theirs before Jerusalem falls."

Bennet looked across the valley at the wall. It appeared to be low until he saw a camel like a dot against it. Suddenly, out from some unseen gate, swiftly moving dots came streaming.

"Turks!" Bennet cried.

Wheeling, they rode as fast as they dared down the slope and lost themselves in the olive trees.

They had come through Bethlehem and were halfway to Nicopolis when they met the first of the crusaders. Barefooted, singing hymns and waving branches of palm, the people swarmed along the road. Among them, but not leading, was Jacques with the blue gonfalon and behind him came Lord Godfrey.

The sight of his master lashed Bennet with the seriousness of what he had done. A squire should be at all times the shadow of his lord, yet he had gone dashing off after another leader. And he had seen Jerusalem—actually nothing more than a gray stone wall, but still Jerusalem—in the company of someone other than the knight he had sworn to serve.

Godfrey came straight on and Bennet met him face to face. The Duke did not speak. His gray eyes remained steadily on the far road. He wore his full mail but no helmet, and his hair shone in the sunlight.

Bennet reined his horse in and turned to ride beside Godfrey. "Sire, I only wanted to see Bethlehem," he faltered.

"Take your place in line," the Duke said quietly.

The boy fell back beside Gareau. The calm order had stung far more than any scolding.

"Don't look so grief-stricken," the troubadour said. "He doesn't doubt your fealty, only your judgment. You young hotheads might have drawn half the Turkish army out after you, and we're not prepared. Look at them!"

Bennet had already looked. The praying, exalted, unarmed pilgrims were a perfect target for Turkish arrows.

"Jerusalem, lift up thine eyes!" they chanted. "Behold the liberator who comes to break thy chains!"

"We won't break them in a day," said Old Barb who had
come up from behind on his mule. "That heathen caliph
has burned all the villages, fired all the wheat fields around
Jerusalem, poisoned the wells. We need manna from heaven
and a good swift rain!"

Bennet couldn't worry over fields or wells. His heart was
too heavy over what he had done to Lord Godfrey.

All day the mass moved slowly over the ancient roads,
and by late afternoon they were just out of range of arrows
from the walls. Tancred and Bennet had seen the wall from
the east, but the main body of the crusaders had come
from the west along the Jaffa Road. Before them lay the
Tower of David, solid stone cemented with mortar. Like
Antioch and Nicaea, Jerusalem also was fortified by a
double wall which had been well repaired by the caliph
while the pilgrims were making their slow approach. Across
the road ran the aqueduct of Roman days, its arches marching from the Valley of Gihon through the Wall of Herod into
the city. Every hill and valley and landmark was a reminder
of the days when the Man had come from Nazareth to teach
peace in Jerusalem.

The camp that night was far different from any made
before. No shelters were put up, no fires built. Most of the
pilgrims spent the evening hours on their knees. None but
the children and the very old slept. They had come to the
end of the journey. Only a wall separated them on this
northwest side of the city from the Via Dolorosa and the
Church of the Resurrection. Bennet, kneeling near Lord
Godfrey, forgot the worries which had beset him. Over the
wall, tomorrow, lay the end of his dream.

CHAPTER FOURTEEN
THE WALLS OF JERUSALEM

It was the sixth of July in 1099 when the crusading army encamped outside the walls of Jerusalem. The city, many felt, would fall miraculously into their hands; but Peter the Hermit said otherwise and the Christians who escaped through the gates backed him up. Iftikar, the caliph, had less than twenty thousand fighting men, but some ten thousand of the citizens had taken up arms along the garrison and there were provisions for a long siege. Machines to cast stones were placed out of sight along the top of the walls. There were barrels of pitch and oil to be heated to boiling and poured down on anyone approaching near enough, and there was the dreaded Greek fire which could be extinguished only with vinegar.

Bennet, on the fringe of the council gathered on a knoll near the Jaffa Road, looked up at the great silent stretch of stone beyond the ditch and tried to imagine these inhuman instruments of war crouched there like beasts in a forest. The city appeared to be very quiet. Somewhere a trumpet called the infidels to prayer in the mosques.

"Their prayers will be short," said the white-bearded hermit who had spoken to Tancred on the Mount of Olives. "When they think your attack is about to begin, they will set fire to the Church of the Resurrection. You must give them no time."

"How can we make an assault when we have no machines of war and no materials to build them?" Raymond asked.

"Take the walls by storm!" Tancred declared. "We have the leather harness of our horses. Splice it into ladders. If we work all night we'll be ready for attack in the morning!"

"By God's will, we'll be ready!" Godfrey declared.

The people standing near took up the cry, and it ran out over the kneeling multitude. The time for prayer was over. Many hands were needed to prepare for the final onslaught.

In Biblical times the valleys and hills around Jerusalem had been covered with flowering gardens and vineyards. Now on the sterile plain and dry mountains there were only scattered clumps of cypress and olive trees and the low growth of terebinth and aloe, and the rhamnus shrub from which the Crown of Thorns had been made. These were torn apart and used as bars and thongs with the leather to form the ladders. No one worked with any great care.

Jerusalem was about to fall and God required only a token effort from His children waiting before the wall.

By the next evening, however, the pilgrims knew that no miracle would deliver the city to them. Although they had outdone themselves in bravery and the outer wall had broken up under their fierce storming, the inner wall remained intact. Battering rams would have to be built and there were no timbers with which to build them.

"Then we'll pull down the churches and use the beams!" Godfrey ordered.

But even those stout cypress logs were not enough, and the rams lay half completed while the crusaders wondered if God had indeed turned against them. Tormented by thirst, stung by the desert sand driven before the hot winds, many of the pilgrims wandered away in search of water and never were seen again. Horses and even camels died on the plains, men dug for themselves what looked like shallow graves and lay in them to draw what comfort they could from the faint moisture of the newly turned earth.

"If the Moslems made a foray against us now, we'd all be butchered," Gareau said one afternoon. "And if it's true that another army is moving out of Egypt to the aid of the caliph——"

Gareau paused, and Bennet raised his head. They were lying in the small shade of the blue tent, inside of which Godfrey and Tancred talked over plans which could not be carried out. Old Barb was approaching on his mule. There were rumors that Barb knew of a secret spring where he and his mule drank in the dead of night, for neither seemed to suffer from thirst.

"Vessels from Genoa!" Barb cried before he was off the mule, and he shrugged and winked so rapidly that the one little hoof remaining on the cap now jumped around and hit him on the chin. "Vessels have come into Jaffa! There's been a battle and some of the ships were destroyed but if we hurry we can save the provisions! Where's Duke Godfrey?"

Godfrey and Tancred were already out of the tent. Immediately the oliphants summoned the other leaders and within an hour a party of three hundred knights and squires were on their way to Jaffa.

Equally as important as the provisions and water were the men who came from the ships, Genoese carpenters and engineers. Gaston of Bearn, an experienced engineer who had made many trips through Palestine, looked at the battle-scarred walls and declared them not to be impregnable. Thirty miles from Jerusalem, he said, was a forest which would yield more than enough logs for the battering rams. Within the hour oxen shod with iron were on their way to the forest, and in a few days they were back with the first hewn timbers.

Then the zeal of the pilgrims became miraculous. All the able-bodied men labored at cutting and hoisting the logs. The sick made water bags out of skins, and the women and children carried the bags to be filled at the Fountain of Elpira on the Damascus Road or at a small brook beyond Bethlehem, seven miles away. Others made coarse needles out of the rhamnus thorns and sewed together more skins to stretch over the battering rams to protect them from fire. The smallest children gathered branches for bundles to be cast flaming over the wall.

Under Gaston's direction, three towers were completed. Each had three levels. On the bottom would be the guides who would do the backbreaking task of pushing the tower up to the walls. On the second and third levels the soldiers would be packed, safe from the enemy. When the tower came near enough to the ramparts, the drawbridge at the highest level would be dropped on to the wide summit of the wall and the soldiers would rush out.

"Now that you are ready for attack, you must sanctify yourselves for the great undertaking," the hermit advised.

The soldiers grumbled at the delay because rumors were growing that the army from Egypt was not far off; but the leaders remembered their blasphemy and doubts of God when other trials were upon them. And so the Moslems were treated to the strange sight of the Westerners letting their fine new engines of war stand idle while they endured a fast of three days. Then, barefooted and bareheaded, led by their priests, singing psalms, they marched entirely around the walls of Jerusalem. The Moslems made a procession of their own on top of the ramparts, shouting and jeering, carrying a rude cross which they insulted in every manner. But the prayers of the Christians only rose higher above the clashing of cymbals and blaring of trumpets— the voice of heaven, said Peter the Hermit, prevailing over the racket of hell.

Great quiet pervaded the camp and the city that night. At Nicaea and Antioch there had been emissaries going back and forth with demands and offers for surrender. At Jerusalem there were none. The fight would be bloody and to the death.

Bennet, wandering about uneasily, came upon Hughette kneeling by herself with her hands clasped over a large rock. Back in Bouillon she had been the little kitchen maid who slipped him something to eat when his escapades made him late for supper at home. She wore rags now, but she looked across at the wall as Mary might have looked at those same rocks of Calvary.

"It's before you now, Bennet."

"Jerusalem?"

"Your knighthood. Right over the wall is the Church of the Resurrection. You said you'd be knighted there."

"We have to take the city first."

Hughette only smiled. Bennet sat down on the rock. They were still there, silent, when the pages ran through the camp with the order to begin formation.

This time there was no wheezing of the oliphants. In the darkness, secretly, the men of Lorraine went to work. Godfrey had built his tower northwest of the wall. The Moslems, watching it go up, had made preparations to defend this section. But now, as quietly as they could, the crusaders took down the tower and carried it piece by piece around to the north across the old Samaria Road and into the Valley of Jehosophat. When the dawn broke the Moslems flocked to the defense of the northwest wall. But where was the enemy? From their new position in the valley the crusaders could see the Turks running like frightened ants around the top of the ramparts.

"If only we could attack now!" Godfrey groaned.

But the fine three-level tower was only a mass of timbers that must be reassembled. For three days and nights the men labored, and the tower was once more erected.

"The Moslems will never touch this!" Gaston cried as he fastened a large gold crucifix to the front of the tower. "Now we are ready!"

And so with the dawn of Thursday, July 14, began the struggle to push the tower to the wall. The Moslem defenders immediately let fly a storm of arrows. In the three days' delay they had made an impenetrable barrier of bound straw and sticks on top of the wall and from this shelter their petraries shot flaming torches against the tower. Bennet, watching with Lord Godfrey from the hill-

side, ran back and forth trying to see through the smoke
and the dust of the falling mortar. The first wall went down
with terrible thunder.

"Sire, we're into Jerusalem!" Bennet cried, dancing up
and down.

But Godfrey shook his head. "No. The inside wall is the
one they really defend. Now the battle begins." And he
looked toward the west where other clouds rose from
Raymond's assault at the Jaffa Gate.

Darkness fell with no victory on either side. Tancred
climbed to Godfrey's lookout and threw himself down on
ground still hot from the day.

"The enemy fights as desperately as we do," he said.
"They know we will annihilate them if we take the city.
We know they will slaughter us to the last man if the vic-
tory goes to them."

"It cannot go to them," Godfrey said grimly. "This is our
last stand. Stay and rest, Tancred. I'll go down and see to
the repair of the tower."

But Tancred was already on his feet. "Robert of Flanders
is going to set up a new assault with me at St. Stephen's
Gate, ready for morning."

"We must not divide our forces further!"

"We're not, my lord. The gate is only a good stone's throw
from the tower. But another assault will force the Moslems
to divide for defense."

Talking together the two went down the long hill, and
Bennet followed. Men who had fought all day were strag-
gling up on the lower slopes and falling asleep as their
heads touched the ground. Beside them, as if on guard,
sat the women who had labored bringing water from Bethlehem, and the children cuddled close to their mothers.
The side of the tower next to the wall had been badly

burned; but there were extra timbers for repair and in the pitch darkness the men labored in shifts, some sleeping while others worked. By dawn, when the oliphants again sounded, the crusaders were ready.

The enemy flew to man their war machines and once again the bundles of flaming sticks and the flints were a raging hail against the tower. The knights, ranged so close together that their shields held over their heads made a continuous ceiling, protected the workmen who strained to push the heavy tower closer to the wall. Behind them the archers and the crossbowmen shot their arrows furiously. Javelins hissed through the air, lances slashed whenever an enemy came near enough.

Godfrey did not watch the battle from a distance today. On the highest level of the tower, where he could dash across the drawbridge the moment it could be let down on to the wall, he wielded his javelin with steady aim. Bennet, down below, saw the brave men of Lorraine, wounded, fall one after another from the tower to be buried under the stones and mortar tumbling before the battering rams. Today there was not even water to give them, for the Moslems, discovering how the soldiers were being supplied, had sent out so many forays that Godfrey had forbidden the women to go again to Bethlehem.

It was noon when Old Barb appeared at the tower and tried to worm his way up the ladder to the higher levels.

"Get back!" the knights cried. "You're only in our way!"

"I wanted to tell Lord Godfrey how it goes with Count Raymond and Tancred," Barb complained as he dropped back beside Bennet. "Not that the news would cheer him. They're having no better success."

A heavy thud hit the tower.

"Greek fire!" someone shouted. "We need more vinegar!"

Old Barb shook his head, shrugged and winked. "I've tramped miles through the vineyards hunting vinegar. There's none to be found."

Fire licked now around the second level, and Bennet leaped at the ladder. A soldier tried to stop him but the boy fought him off. Lord Godfrey was up there, surrounded by the Greek fire. What a squire could do in the face of those murderous flames was something Bennet did not think out. He only knew he had to be beside his master.

Somehow he gained the two flights and squirmed out on the floor. The smoke, closed in by the roof and the three sides of the tower, was a choking mass. The side next to the wall was being eaten away by the flames and through the gaps the nimbly fighting figures of the Moslems could be seen. Jacques was there, holding the blue gonfalon which he would plant on the ramparts with the first assault. Beside him was Godfrey, pale, his hair dark with sweat and grime, watching with hopeless patience as the flames ate at the timbers. If the crusade had had any one leader, it had been Godfrey. He had inspired and browbeaten the army into advancing to this point. And now it seemed that the Greek fire, which could be quenched only by the vinegar they did not have, was about to turn him away in defeat.

Suddenly, framed in the fiery gap in the timbers, two terrible hags appeared. They had climbed out on the wall and they stood waving their bony arms as they shouted incantations at the gold crucifix on the tower which neither the flames nor the arrows had touched all through the course of the battle. As their weird voices rose, the hissing of lances and snap of arrows died away. The army, desperately tired, discouraged, sickened by the sight of their brothers-in-arms falling dead and wounded, seemed to go suddenly limp. Even Godfrey's shield fell clattering on the burning timbers. If the Moslems had rushed forward in that moment, the crusaders would have been driven from the gates of Jerusalem.

Bennet could not watch his master go down in defeat. Staggering in the smoke, he struggled through the motionless soldiers to the open side of the tower facing the plain.

"God, don't let it happen!" he sobbed, and because he could not bear the horror of the battlefield he looked far beyond it to the rolling hill where he and the Lord of Bouillon had stood yesterday.

A different figure was there now on the brow of the hill, a knight in snow-white armor and mounted on a white horse. The visor of the helmet was in place and his face could not be seen, but he was unmistakably one of the knights who had appeared so miraculously at Antioch and turned the tide of the battle.

"Master!" Bennet screamed. "Look! On the hill!"

Everyone in the hot little enclosure turned. Down on the field the soldiers turned, following the pointing arms. The battering ram stopped in the act of a blow, the witches swallowed their screaming. The wounded sat up to look and the weary knights stood with their lances in their hands.

Godfrey stepped to the open side of the chamber.

"St. George!" he cried, and his voice carried far. "St. George the Martyr has come to lead us! Forward, men of Lorraine! Storm the walls!"

A mighty cheer went up, weariness fell from the knights like a cast-off buckler, and the foot soldiers started up with energy. Godfrey waved his sword before the flaming wall.

"Let down the drawbridge! Jacques, the gonfalon!"

The drawbridge which was the whole fiery side of the tower fell with a mighty thunder in a bridge to the top of the wall.

"Now forward!" Godfrey shouted. "It is the will of God!"

Not a man hesitated. But the timbers had been gutted by the fire and as Jacques, the first to cross, stepped out the beam cracked under his weight. He had only time to toss the banner to Godfrey before he disappeared in the smoke. The duke leaped across the gaping hole, but in his armor he also was too heavy for the weakened beams. He would have fallen after Jacques except for the eager hands of his knights. The gonfalon, however, had tumbled into the fire. In their anxiety for Godfrey's safety the knights paid no attention.

But Bennet saw the blue disappear. The gonfalon must not be lost, the army would move forward only so long as they could see the banner. Laurent had died holding up the gonfalon. So had Leroy, and now Jacques. All along the wall the knights and soldiers would watch for their standard to lead the charge against the wall. Not seeing it, they would hesitate and the Moslems would have all the chance they needed to drive them back.

Bennet slipped down the ladder to the second level and finally to the ground. The Greek fire burned in tongues around the tower and the soldiers were trying to beat it out. Bennet fought his way toward the wall. The hot dust seared his throat, stones fell, and there was a puddle of hot oil that had been poured down from above. A shower of molten lead hit the ground near him.

"Get back!" a knight shouted. "Nobody can live in there!"

But the boy could see the blue gonfalon where it had slipped down between the stones, dirty and scorched but not yet in flames. Yanking the staff loose, he gathered the cloth into his arms. There was a leather ladder dangling from somewhere up on the wall very close to the drawbridge, and he caught hold of it.

"Boy, don't do that!" the knight shouted again. "It won't hold!"

The ladder did almost break under his weight and it was almost impossible to hang on to the heavy banner; but slowly, one stubborn step after another, Bennet dragged himself up.

He came out beside the drawbridge. The wall was thirty feet wide, barricaded with bundles of sticks and straw now flaming from the darts thrown by the knights. A yelling mob of Moslems surrounded a mangonel, its great timber arm swung back with a beam soaked in pitch ready to cast at the tower; but when they saw the boy, alone, leap to the drawbridge and unfurl the gonfalon, they were too astounded to move.

"Come on, knights of Bouillon!" Bennet shouted across the flaming bridge.

They answered in a mighty roar. Throwing down their shields on top of the flames, they made a safe passage for Lord Godfrey and then pushed after him. The army, seeing the gonfalon on top of the wall, charged with new determination.

"It is the will of God!" they cried.

The shout reached Tancred's men at the Gate of St. Stephen, echoed around the wall to Raymond at the Jaffa Gate, and to them all it was the cry of victory. Nothing could withstand the onslaught.

It was a Friday never to be forgotten in history, that fifteenth of July in 1099. At three o'clock in the afternoon —the very hour in which Christ had given up His life for the redemption of this city and for all mankind—the crusaders poured over the ramparts.

And on the wall, supported by a ragged, dirty, triumphant boy, waved the blue gonfalon of Bouillon.

CHAPTER FIFTEEN
THE BLUE GONFALON

The narrow streets of Jerusalem ran red with blood that day. On the wide paving stones where Jesus had walked the crusaders tramped with heavy vengeance, searching out the Moslems and pursuing them into their temples where they cut them down as if these marble floors were another battlefield. The Christians of the city, fearful that they might be mistaken for the enemy and slaughtered before they could identify themselves, also gathered in their churches and prayed aloud. The sound turned the soldiers back at the doors. When evening came there were no Turkish horns to call the infidels to worship. Only the Angelus rang out over the battered walls.

Bennet had followed Lord Godfrey all day and when the Angelus rang they stopped where they were to say the short prayers. They were in a section of the Via Dolorosa, the way Our Lord had walked to Calvary. The street, perhaps ten feet wide, was flanked by stone buildings with four arches curving overhead as if they were needed up there to keep the buildings apart. Farther along a series of low steps spanned the little thoroughfare.

Impressed by the holy place, the boy took a long time to finish his prayers and when he looked up he saw that the duke was watching him as if he had not noticed his squire for a long time. The beautiful jeweled cross he had worn from France still hung on his powerful, naked chest, his long sword was at his side, but his tunic was as ragged and battle-stained as Bennet's own.

Abruptly he opened the crusader's purse at his belt and took out a tiny object wrapped in a bit of silk. Unwrapped, it lay in his palm—the crude little cross Bennet had made of red dogwood twigs back at Clermont.

"Remember it, boy?"

"I didn't know you'd kept it, Sire."

"Remember how Gareau talked about the 'great, compelling dream' on the way to Clermont? This has been the symbol of it. And now the dream is realized." He laid the tiny cross in Bennet's hand. "You've earned your spurs, boy. If you wish to spend your first night in Jerusalem in preparation, I'll give you the accolade tomorrow morning."

"In the Church of the Holy Sepulchre, Sire?"

Lord Godfrey smiled. "Wherever you like."

Bennet tightened his fingers over the little cross while memories rushed upon him—his mother begging him not to go on crusade, his father fiercely defending his son's right to go, Hughette's father who wanted to be anything but a tanner and her mother lying under stones piled to keep the jackals away. For the few like himself who had reached Jerusalem the sacrifice had been justified. He raised his head, wishing he could tell all this to his master; but Godfrey, with the step of a man who feels a great weight on his shoulders, was walking on up the wide, shallow steps where Christ had dragged His cross.

Against the stone wall Hughette stood, her dark eyes shining. She wore a torn robe she had picked up from some Turkish woman and on her feet were outlandish sandals, but her smile was the same as when she had known first about the great, compelling dream.

"I heard what he said, Bennet."

The boy walked slowly over to her. He had grown, but so had Hughette and her head came to the top of his shoulder.

"I wish you had colors to give me tomorrow, Hughette."

Hughette smiled shyly. She turned her head and her hand slipped up the wall to lie in a small hollow. "Do you know what this is, Bennet? It's the place where Our Lord laid His hand to rest before He started up these steps. He must have been very tired, carrying His cross." Her eyes followed the figure of the Lord of Bouillon plodding in the distance. "He's tired too. They'll make him governor of Jerusalem now —not king. I heard him tell Count Raymond that he would never wear a crown in the city where his Master had worn a crown of thorns. But he will rule. And you know why, Bennet." She smiled straight into his eyes. "Because you were first on the wall with the blue gonfalon!"

"Lord Godfrey is the proper one to govern! They couldn't choose anyone else!" Bennet said gruffly, but he couldn't keep back a proud smile.

Hughette laughed. Then, hand in hand, they wandered up the wide steps after the vanishing figure of the new governor of Jerusalem.

At sunset Bennet went to begin his vigil in the rocky chamber hewn out so long ago by Joseph of Arimathea to be his own tomb. The outer chamber of the tomb had, in the beginning, been reserved for the mourners. Now it was filled with kneeling people waiting their turn to approach the small inner chamber with the long stone ledge on which Christ's body had lain. Bennet, watching them in the candle-light, found it difficult to pray. He couldn't think about himself. He saw instead how the women came like Mary of Magdala to the tomb, touched the great stone which had sealed the chamber and was now rolled aside, and kissed the sacred ledge. No sound but the shuffling feet disturbed the silence. Sometime through the night Gareau came in, and Old Barb with his cap hugged tight. Seeing Bennet, they worked their way over beside him and knelt, praying and watching.

At dawn the boy left the church and returned ready for the ceremony of knighthood. Now he wore the white shirt of purity, the robe crimson as the blood he might pour out to serve God and guard His church, the long brown trunk hose like the earth to which he must return, and the white coif on his head to signify his stainless soul. Lord Godfrey, in full and polished armor but without his helmet, stood by to vest him in new mail. As a squire Bennet had received the hauberk. In knighthood was added the new shield upon which he might paint his own design, the helmet and gauntlets, and finally a naked sword. Then Lord Godfrey touched him on the shoulder with his sword and gave him the kiss of peace.

Hughette, in white with a soft blue veil, came forward smiling in the candlelight.

"I have no colors, Sir Knight, because I'm not a noble lady," she whispered. "But I knew you would earn the blue of Bouillon. Lord Godfrey's lady gave it to me at home for you. I carried it from France!"

And to his new and shining sword she fastened a blue scarf.

Godfrey beckoned to a knight who came holding the banner of Bouillon. It was the old, tattered one they had carried from France, the one that had gone down with Laurent and Leroy and Jacques, finally to be hoisted in triumph on the Jerusalem wall. Lord Godfrey took the staff and set it before Bennet.

"You will bear my standard, Sir Knight! Defend it well!" he said, and he took Bennet's fingers in the brand-new glove and pressed them around the staff. Inside the glove was the little red twig cross.

The boy could not speak. The dream had been realized, and more. In a swimming haze he saw Hughette and Lord Godfrey, and behind them Gareau and Old Barb smiling at him, and the priest raising his hand in blessing. Bennet stood very tall and straight, the new and staunch defender of the blue gonfalon of Bouillon.